THE RIVER SWIMMER

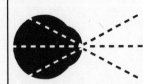

This Large Print Book carries the
Seal of Approval of N.A.V.H.

THE RIVER SWIMMER

NOVELLAS

JIM HARRISON

THORNDIKE PRESS

A part of Gale, Cengage Learning

Detroit • New York • San Francisco • New Haven, Conn • Waterville, Maine • London

GALE
CENGAGE Learning®

LIBRARY OF CONGRESS CATALOGING-IN-PUBLICATION DATA

Harrison, Jim, 1937–
    [Short stories. Selections]
    The river swimmer : novellas / by Jim Harrison. — Large Print edition.
        pages cm. — (Thorndike Press Large Print Core)
    ISBN 978-1-4104-5805-6 (hardcover) — ISBN 1-4104-5805-9 (hardcover)
    1. Short stories, American. 2. American fiction. 3. Large type books. I. Title.
    PS3558.A67R58 2013
    813'.54—dc23   2013001442

Published in 2013 by arrangement with Grove/Atlantic, Inc.

Printed in the United States of America
1 2 3 4 5 6 7 17 16 15 14 13

To Andrew and Anna

CONTENTS

THE LAND OF UNLIKENESS

■ ■ ■ ■

PART I

■ ■ ■ ■

CHAPTER 1

Clive awoke before dawn in a motel in Ypsilanti, Michigan, thinking that it was altogether possible that every woman in the world was married to the wrong man. He was sixty and hadn't been married in twenty years but his divorce was still the starkest rupture in his life. Afterward his fire was doused, or so he thought, and he had quit being a painter and had become an art history professor, an emissary, appraiser, and cultural handyman. In actuality he had allowed time to slur reality and the break was far from clean. The year before the divorce his final show at a New York gallery had been declared by a *Times* critic to be "absurdly decorative," the kiss of death for an abstract painter and also a kiss good-bye with a gallery that had only sold two of the thirty paintings and those heavily discounted to one of Clive's few collectors.

Ypsilanti wasn't a destination, to be sure,

but a stop on his way to northern Michigan to look after his semiblind eighty-five-year-old mother while his sister made her first trip to Europe. His sister had chided him on the phone that he had admitted to more than thirty trips to Europe while she hadn't been once. This wouldn't have been possible but he had been put on a three-month leave of absence by his Ivy League university for an unfortunate incident that had involved minimal but disastrous self-defense. During the annual public lecture that was part of his obligation for his endowed chair in the humanities a dozen members of a group called the Art Tarts had rushed up on the stage and their leader, a thin young woman of Amazonian height, had thrown a canister of yellow paint on his favorite suit (Savile Row) and then began rapping on his chest with a sharp knuckle while screaming "Sexist cocksucker!" He pushed her away and she tumbled backward off the podium, gave her head a nasty crack, and broke her collarbone. Fortunately for Clive the lecture had been videotaped, though the dean dissuaded him from pursuing an assault charge. She pursued one, but her contingency lawyer had seen the videotape and told her that he couldn't win her a dime.

Above all else, including a list of neurotic

disorders, marital and academic difficulties, Clive was a man of surpassing good humor and amazing memory. He remembered everyone's name across the board from society people to grocery clerks to janitors and cleaning women. As a child he had been fascinated by names and had kept a name journal throughout his life. In his side work appraising art — nineteenth-century American art was his specialty — for estate, insurance, or divorce purposes, he knew the names of a dozen doormen on the Upper East Side of Manhattan. Always a liberal he insisted on being called by his first name so he was greeted by them as "Mister Clive."

After a twelve-hour drive and a bitterly stupid late meal in Ypsilanti he was susceptible to his only two current anger items. First was his ruined favorite suit which literally made him see yellow. It was irreplaceable mostly because he had lost nearly 70 percent of the value of his modest portfolio in the economic plunge. This was due to receiving stock tips from a hedge fund stalwart who himself had lost a couple of billion. The man had been apoplectic for a year because he had bought many paintings at exorbitant prices and now had to pay his long-term wife half their value in their divorce settlement.

The night of modest indigestion led him to question why an ordinary mom-and-pop restaurant would put a big amount of rosemary, currently America's most overused herb, in their meat loaf. This led to his prime source of anger which he tended to keep private except with a few friends. It was greed. Unmitigated cupidity. Despite having quit painting twenty years before, Clive was a romantic idealist about art. He had noted beginning in the past two and a half decades the growing percentage of people who when they talked about art were only talking about the art market and its confetti of price tags. Some days it was up to 100 percent. He had long ago given up making pointed remarks about the fact that art and the art market were two entirely different things. Clive was not widely read in the field of socioeconomics or the problem would have been clearer. Such academic prose was utterly without aesthetic merit and this quality was demanded in something as simple as this money obsession. It was a brutish crime indeed and far from the ideals of a boy of ten, who had been dropped off at the Big Rapids Public Library to study art books with goose bumps while his parents shopped at the grocery and hardware store and picked up feed at the grain

16

elevator. The final blasphemous straw, though it wasn't a painting, was a bid of twenty-eight million dollars for a single chair at the Yves Saint Laurent belongings auction in Paris. Curiously, his many French and Italian friends and acquaintances rarely spoke of money. They didn't necessarily have better taste but open discussions about money were apparently in bad form.

It was only 5 a.m. and he didn't want to wait two hours for Zingerman's to open in the neighboring city of Ann Arbor in order to buy intriguing food supplies. He would call in and do a FedEx order, which would irritate his penurious mother. He had wanted to dine at Zingerman's Roadhouse the evening before but was absolutely sure he would run into someone he knew. He had begun his teaching career at the University of Michigan and even though that was more than fifteen years before, the idea of explaining his recent mudbath to an old colleague was unacceptable. The Internet and pestilential e-mail ensured that the gossip would have made its way around. The *New York Times* had run a very small item but the *Post* had run a photo of him staring down cross-eyed at the paint on his suit.

All of these annoyances passed with the

pressure of leaving early enough to miss the rush hour and the more than overwhelming glories of burgeoning spring. Since childhood he had favored May above all other months and driving north a couple of hundred miles to what was left of the old farm was curiously enlivening in its variations of diminishing spring, much stronger in the south, but still there farther north with budding hardwoods and a distinct emerging green in pastures with loitering black and white Holsteins, all of which began to purge his mind of the enervations of his livelihood. When he turned east on a gravel road between Big Rapids and Reed City he stopped beside a marsh with the car windows rolled down and listened to the trilling cacophony of hundreds of red-winged blackbirds, and on the other side of the road the more dulcet calls of meadowlarks. He recalled with immoderate reverence his burgeoning love at age ten for looking at paintings and listening to classical music, the lack of *mind* in his pleasure. How wonderful it was to love something without the compromise of language.

CHAPTER 2

For reasons of clarity Clive liked to dice his life into paragraphs in his journal, kept since his teens. All of this writing, not to speak of his obsessive reading of the best in literature, had the benefit of teaching him to write well. One of the rawest paragraphs, however, came about after the collapse of his painting life when he was a graduate student at the University of Michigan. A professor had loved an essay Clive had written about Blumenschein, a painter of the Taos school, and had said, "It's a good thing you quit! You write too well for a painter. Painters don't write well."

"What about Robert Motherwell?" Clive had asked, always irked at such didactic statements.

"Motherwell is passé," the professor said, fiddling with his meerschaum, then beginning one of his geometric doodles. Many of his graduate students referred to him as

"Mister Doodles."

Clive had merely nodded and left the office with a smile. After all, he had received high and prophetic praise for his Blumenschein essay. Despite an eighty-year slump, Blumenschein prices eventually rose to as much as a million, obviously a matter of no consequence to the long dead artist. On his way to have a cup of coffee after the enervating meeting with the professor, Clive had stopped to make a few notes in his pocket notebook, which would later be transferred to his journal in the form of a terse paragraph.

I've been told that Motherwell is passé. Just the other day at the coffee shop I told a PhD candidate in music how much I enjoyed reading Steinbeck. He snorted and chortled as if he had caught me masturbating while picking my nose. "No one takes Steinbeck seriously," he hissed. This young man is writing his dissertation on a composer named Harold Arlen with whom I'm not familiar. In big cities and in university centers in the hinterlands the air guitarists are forever making decisions on who has become passé. They remind me of certain patrons of my favorite NYC jazz

20

clubs like the Five Spot or Slugs, ultra-hip guys who appear to believe that the music of the performers depends on their presence.

He missed the turn to his mother's driveway, perhaps on purpose. He wasn't ready yet and never would be, he thought. "What is this?" he said aloud in the car. It had been three years since he had been back home and seen the twenty-acre thicket his mother had planted forty years before after his father's death. In the three years of over-average rainfall the thicket had grown exponentially, with a riot of small pale green leaves flipping the undersides in the stiff late morning wind. The thicket was her retreat from the peopled world, which she found unsavory in nearly all respects. In the interim his mother had visited him with his sister Margaret twice in New York City which had meant a couple of days of dreary plodding after her in the Museum of Natural History. They would stay with him in his modest apartment on West End Avenue which he could no longer afford, the rent having risen 500 percent in seventeen years. To his complaints the rental agent had thrown up his hands and said "Tough titty." His mother's failing vision had limited her somewhat to pressing her nose against the glass cases of seemingly thousands of dead, stuffed birds and saying, "My goodness." Margaret had warned him on the phone that after leading her out at dawn to one of her bird-watching sites he would have to keep alert for when she blew the dog whistle so that he could fetch her when the time came. This had come from a phone call only days before and in his current despondency he rather liked the idea of being beckoned by a dog whistle.

He drove another mile past his mother's house down the gravel road, refusing the weight of sentiment in his boyhood land-scape. He was distracted again by the thought of the whale skeleton hanging from the ceiling in the huge hall of the Field Museum in Chicago. It was normally a personal taboo to think of painting anything but he couldn't help himself when it came to the whale. He would lead his mother to a bench, perhaps in a room full of unattrac-tive stuffed snakes, tell her to stay there, and then go out for a cigarette. On coming back in he would stop and stare upward at the whale pondering a holographic painting of the immense ribs from a point of view inside the capacious rib cage. He had mildly fantasized finding a room somewhere and doing the painting despite his twenty-year avowal never to paint again.

He turned around in the driveway of his high school girlfriend Laurette. The present owner had done, to his eye, a wretched job of gentrifying the farmhouse with flouncy dormers and copper flashing on the roof edges. The natural redwood siding looked out of place so far from California and the lawn now was absurdly manicured with geometrical perennial beds. Gone were the lilac groves and the ancient tire swing where Laurette would sing the Disney song "Zip-a-dee-doo-dah" while swinging ever higher. To be frank he had never been acknowledged as Laurette's boyfriend and she thoroughly ignored him during school hours but they had grown up as lonely farm kid neighbors and were close outside of the small high school where Laurette was part of the *in* group. His singular period of acceptance came every fall at football where the usual fascist coach had made him into a middle linebacker and though the school had a limited talent pool there were a dozen big strong farm boys, usually enough to trash the urban schools. After football season he went back to being just plain Frenchy because in the thrall of art in the ninth grade he had cut the small bill off a cap and made it into a beret. Nicknames arrived like that. His friend Luke Carlson who was six foot four and 230 pounds at age fourteen was called Big Dork because he had a large penis. This was embarrassing to Luke because he and his family were devout Lutherans and any vaguely sexual reference in school would make Luke and his very large sisters blush in unison.

After turning around Clive found himself driving toward his mother's at less than twenty miles per hour and laughed. He had always treated her with affection and nonchalance despite her needling, but a mother can be a fearsome creature. Clive admitted to himself that his mother had disliked Laurette for the suffering she had caused her son. Laurette had spent her teens as a relentlessly petulant young woman. His sister Margaret who was five years younger than Clive always referred to Laurette as "the bitch." Laurette had actually laughed with her friends when he was fourteen and selling his petite landscapes at a table at a county fair for five bucks, having made lovely frames out of beech with his dad's miter box. A well-heeled matron had bought three of his landscapes, then popped out the paintings on the table and walked off saying, "I only wanted the frames." Clive had been enraged and sailed the paintings off toward the pig barn. Laurette and her friends laughed and Clive stormed off to the parking lot and the Model A Ford he had bought for fifty bucks. On his way he picked up an *in* crowd lout and put the struggling young man on a merry-go-round pony to the laughter of the crowd. Farm boys don't try to be strong but their labor makes them that way. That evening Laurette had dropped off his three landscapes saying that she had wiped the pig poop off one. Clive was still angry but grateful. She chided him about bullying her friend. Clive didn't want to be strong, he wanted to be a slender aesthete.

CHAPTER 3

Lunch was thankfully short. At Mother's house you ate what was served and in the proportions she had decided were appropriate. In this case it was a cup of cottage cheese, homemade applesauce from a tree out back, and half a sandwich from a delicious ham a neighbor had smoked from their own little smoke shack the neighbor had bought and helped disassemble in the late sixties after Clive's father's death. As a lagniappe Clive was offered a tiny lemon bar. When Mother left for her nap he went outside and sat on the deck with Margaret.

"Lunch was slim. She ate nine lemon bars last evening after dinner and today she wants to diet again."

"My God, nine?" Clive said without interest. His mother has been on a diet for decades.

"She said she was going to die anyway so nine lemon bars didn't matter but this morning she only wanted a poached egg and Ry-Krisp. I hope you can poach eggs soft but not too soft." Margaret laughed at her brother's immediate discomfort.

"I've never poached an egg," he mumbled.

"I'll give you a lesson this afternoon. Where did you get those beautiful trousers?"

"In Florence last October. Firenze they call it." Clive specialized in picking up the odd piece of clothing on his dozens of European trips. A handwoven and tailored light summer sport coat from Cordoba, a bulky corduroy sport coat from Calabria, a half dozen pairs of linen trousers in Nice and a half dozen linen shirts from the same tailor, cream colored and off white, a butcher's leather vest from western Burgundy, brogans from a shoemaker in Dublin which were resoled every seven years. At a party after a Lincoln Center function Tommy Hilfiger had said, "My God, who dresses you? Fabulous." Clive never wore neckties under the private conviction that all of the political and financial mischief in the nation was created by men who wore neckties.

"You're in for it, kiddo. I taped the instructions to the refrigerator." Margaret laughed again. "But then what's a month? As a New Yorker you'll be pissed that you have to lead her out to a bird-watching site at six a.m.

after coffee. I made a map and a numbered list of the sites."

"Thank you. I usually get up at seven a.m. anyway," he lied, idly wondering why people lied about money, alcohol, and when they got up in the morning. At least rural Midwesterners lied about sleeping hours, having been relentlessly taught that "the early bird gets the worm." Rural Midwesterners were given to getting up in the dark and patiently waiting for daylight. At least with his father there were chores to be done. The cows and the remaining old draft horse had to be fed. Clive would pitch down hay for the half dozen Holsteins and Jerry, the draft horse, the remnant of a team that had been retired after their first tractor had been purchased when Clive was six.

Margaret helped him carry his luggage up to his boyhood room at the back of the house on the second story. Clive hadn't stayed in the room in more than a decade, preferring a motel in Reed City for his visits while his mother was still on the warpath. Only in her early eighties did she begin to mellow and during the last visit to New York City with Margaret she had grasped his hand across the kitchen table when talking about how well his father had danced the polka.

"I was the envy of every woman over Ralph's dancing. You better believe he raised his knees high at the polka and in perfect time to the music."

She was definitely never a hand-holder. Margaret left in a merry huff over toting one of his too heavy Moroccan leather suitcases upstairs. He noted how happy she had become after her divorce three years before in Chicago where she had run a laboratory in a big hospital. Clive had loathed her dot commer husband, a technocratic oaf of which there were many, though the couple had produced two fine sons now in their midtwenties. His mother's constant complaint was that she would likely die without great-grandchildren since Margaret's boys seemed ill inclined toward marriage and his own estranged daughter, Sabrina, was definitely not marriage material. Sabrina was working toward a PhD in earth sciences, whatever that was, at the University of Washington in Seattle. This seemed to him extraordinary for a rich girl who had never acted spoiled. Their moment of disaffection had come three years ago when they were eating in Babbo on the eve of his ex-wife's fourth marriage in Santa Monica, where she had a house off San Vicente.

"Your mother is buying husbands like

trinkets," he had said idly while drinking a full bottle of Amarone. Sabrina had gone for a couple of glasses of budget Friuli.

"Dad, what an unspeakably asshole thing to say. She needs the love you never gave her, that's for sure. You were all about ambition. You didn't even come to graduation."

Sabrina threw down two one-hundred-dollar bills, a habit of her mother's, this throwing money. He had missed her Wellesley graduation because he had been near Saint-Rémy, France, appraising the collection of an American man on the verge of divorce. The man was itching to have a couple of Matisses declared bogus to save settlement money. Sabrina had gone out the door leaving her veal chop untouched and his ensuing letters and phone calls were unanswered. He had taken the veal chop home to the apartment. Sabrina had visited her grandmother a couple of times a year, staying in this very room he thought.

Maybe it was all about delusions of integrity. In his own twenties he had thought overmuch about not compromising when no one was asking him to compromise. At that age a specific rigidity seemed necessary to isolate yourself from your own confusion and to invent the person you were to become. Sabrina and her grandmother had always had an open level of communication based on their mutual obsession with the natural world. He had nothing of the kind with either of them since they both were singularly disinterested in his own passion for art.

He sat on a reading chair beside the back window of his boyhood room. Margaret had thoroughly cleaned the room but had not quite expunged the mustiness of disuse. Above the antique iron bedstead painted white with brass knobs on the posts were three of his early landscapes with only *Pond at Dawn* showing any talent, his having caught the rising mist off the water and the curious blur of lily pads, an effect cribbed from Monet. Of far more interest to him were the wavering distortions offered by the antique glass back window and the rusty torn screen behind it. A spider was trying to extricate one of its eight feet from the screen which gave Clive a feeling of uneasiness so he stepped through the open door into the hall. He tried to ignore two of his early paintings Margaret had hung in the hall but gave up and looked at them closely. He mildly liked the one of Jerry the draft horse's head, but he attributed this to sentimentality. The other was an amateurish portrait of Dad's green John Deere tractor made at his father's request. There was too much green, as his father had parked the tractor in front of a grove of lilacs which had been toward the end of the blooming period, so that the flowers hung limp and desiccated. There had been a mild argument with his father, a firm supporter, who had ordered Clive's first twelve-dollar watercolor set from the Montgomery Ward catalog. His father wanted the tractor, lilacs, and all of the backdrop including the farm implement shed in perfect focus, which had put the twelve-year-old artist in a state of high dudgeon but ultimately had been wonderful. Clive had patiently explained that a painting wasn't a snapshot. A photo can be okay but that's not how we see. When we look at things we don't put the entirety of the surroundings of what we're looking at in focus. He and his father had had a wonderful time walking around the barnyard looking at things. His father had agreeably noted that when you looked up at a swallow's nest under the barn's eaves the wooden slats of the barn aren't in focus and neither is the metal roof. When you are looking at a particular hen in a flock of thirty chickens the thirty are certainly not seen in photographic detail. When Jerry lifts his huge head from the water trough you see the water dripping from his muzzle in the glint of the sun for a moment and that's all you see. Out of his implicit sense of fairness Clive had said that great photographers were more likely to imitate painters than vice versa.

Clive turned in the hall and stared at the source of his early life's work. The hall window was part of a door that looked out at the twenty-acre thicket. He had been a scant five years old when his father had taken the door from an abandoned country church a few miles down the road cushioning the pickup bed with empty burlap potato sacks. Clive had tagged along in his miniature OshKosh overalls with saggy suspenders and was a little worried that his father was stealing. The upstairs door was necessary because a maiden aunt who had a phobia about fire was living with them, thus his father had installed the second-floor door and a wooden staircase down the back of the house in case the aunt had to escape a burning house. That was fifty-five years ago and the sloppily built staircase was gone and the door was there now nailed shut.

It was the door that brought Clive as a child through the portals of the mystery of vision. The outer edges were dozens of pieces of beveled leaded glass and the boy

33

looking through each fragment was given a peculiar distorted vision of the back forty, now a thicket and pasture gone wild. At sixty Clive knelt on the floor and peered through the lower separate small panes as if he were five again. A bird flew by and startled him and he suddenly stood up feeling an uncomfortable itch in his head from this time travel. On his way downstairs he recalled a lecture he had given about the origins of painting, and how the child makes squares of reality with his fingers and peers through the square at the mysterious world, or in a house moves his head left or right to change the view of the world through panes of glass. He had ended the lecture contentiously with a quote from the literary critic Randall Jarrell, who had written to his wife, "What a pity that we didn't live in an age when painters were still interested in the world." This naturally pissed off the abstract expressionists in his New York audience but having abandoned painting Clive no longer had any territory to protect. He was up for anyone doing what they wished as long as they weren't all doing the same thing. Back in the seventies and eighties he thought there must have been twenty thousand abstract painters in the art schools and universities throughout the country. He had noted something similar when as a morning ritual he listened to Garrison Keillor's *Writer's Almanac* with sketches and birth dates of writers' lives finishing with a contemporary poem. As an obsessive reader he had noted that novels, stories, and the poems Garrison read all tended to deal with etiolated suburban ironies. Maybe in unison with the painters there also had been twenty thousand MFAs in fiction and poetry? In any event he had become bored with his thinking. To even say aloud the truncated phrase "the arts" had become a big cotton ball in the mouth and such inanities as "a rich cultural heritage" were sheer torture. He had forgotten who had said "Art cannot survive the abstraction of it." In his old room he had studiously avoided looking at the bookcase on the far side of the bed.

He decided to take a walk and tiptoed through the living room past his mother, who was dozing upright on the sofa with a large book about raptors on her lap. He paused at the refrigerator to filch a piece of the delicious ham and at the same moment he heard his mother's voice.

"Son, that ham is for Margaret's going-away breakfast and for a sandwich I'll make her to pack along. You can't tell how they're going to feed her overseas."

He fled in haste. He had had the urge to do a reconnaissance of the thicket while Margaret was still here in order to ask her any pertinent questions, but in his hurry he'd unfortunately forgotten to take along her map of the thicket pinned by a magnet to the refrigerator door, or the aerosol can of mosquito dope Margaret had advised. There had recently been a heady item in the *New York Times* on how it was important to take a pee before driving because the biological urgency of having to pee will adumbrate your driving skills. Chewing the ham and his mother's voice made him forget the map and mosquito dope.

First he walked out to the gravel road for a clear view of north and south and the sun's afternoon to get his bearings. South was diverting because he could see Laurette's house a mile distant, also a farm lane lined with Lombardy poplars on the west side, the scene of a memory that was still curiously raw after forty-plus years. It irritated him that the farm was still part of his character despite how much he had resisted its tagging along behind his life. The irresistible memory, with a remnant of rawness akin to the wound left behind by a tooth extraction, burst into his consciousness with the sight of the tree-bordered farm lane before he began walking the thicket path. Two nights before graduation he had dropped his date off in Reed City, then was flagged down by Laurette and several of her friends under a streetlight. It had been the traditional "girls' night out" for those in the *in* crowd and they all were a bit drunk and stoned on the weak local pot called Indiana Red. They all shrieked "Frenchy" when they normally would have ignored his passing car. The problem was that the girl who was supposed to give Laurette a ride home was out of it and was Clive willing? Of course. The group had been skinny dipping and Laurette's hair was still wet and she smelled pleasantly like lake water. Her head lolled a bit and her normally crisp voice was a little slurred. They chatted like they had been doing since kindergarten.

"Did you have a hot date with Tania?" she asked without interest.

"Of course. We fucked like minks," he teased.

"You didn't!" she laughed.

"Then we didn't if you say so." Clive and Tania had had a mild coupling. She was somewhat of a hippie, the movement having invaded the outback in 1968, and she and Clive were the only members of the class who actually read books so the relationship of the two was thought to be natural to others.

"Just think. Six hundred acres under the plow." They were passing her boyfriend Keith's family farm where a half dozen silos gleamed in the moonlight.

"Tell it to someone who gives a shit."

"You're just a poor boy who's jealous." She was pissed. "You don't want me to tie the knot with Keith in July? You're invited."

"I'll pass."

"We're lifelong friends and you won't come to my wedding?" Now she was teary.

"I can't deal with bourgeois spectacles." He loved the word *bourgeois* and overused it.

She wanted to talk so he pulled off down the farm lane between their houses. She had half a joint in her purse which she lit and he drew a pint of peppermint schnapps from under the car seat.

"We haven't kissed in years." She coughed.

"It was in the eighth grade. You needed me for practice." The French kissing had taken place on the porch swing in August at her place. She had hooted with laughter when he got a hard-on, slapping at it, which was painful.

"Well, this will be our last chance so we

could make out a little. Of course you know me and Keith have gone all the way."

He certainly didn't want to hear this from the love of his life though he had suspected it and heard rumors. Nothing is a secret in small town schools. He had a lump in his throat when he swigged from the schnapps bottle. She drank more deeply and he moved toward her on the capacious front seat of the car. They embraced tightly and kissed so that many years later his taste buds could recall the peculiar mix of flavors of pot and schnapps. When he ran his hands across her bottom and his favorite green skirt that she wore his hands paused feeling no panties line.

"I couldn't find my panties after swimming." She laughed a bit manically and her laughter increased when he boldly, he thought, pushed her skirt up to her waist. "You always wanted to paint me nude and now you don't have your paints. Keep your hands to yourself, buster." She reached a hand up and pushed the button to the dome light. "Here's the other side," she said turning over.

He had become dizzy having forgotten to breathe. She had drawn her knees up and was leaning against the passenger side door with a glittery smile. Her pubis was clearly visible and like all burgeoning painters he was taking mental photos.

"Get yours out and I might just jerk it."

He did and moved toward her. Her hand was rough and a little frantic.

"Your pecker is bigger than Keith's. It's not fair."

"You'll live with it."

"All men's dicks should be the same," she insisted.

"There's no democracy in the arts or in life," he muttered, close to coming off.

"You always have to bring up that art bullshit," she said, taking a firmer grip and he was finished. She grabbed tissues from her purse, wiped her hand, then threw the tissues at his face. She slumped back and closed her eyes. He was bewildered staring at her crotch and thighs. He was still erect but wondered if it was ethical to slip it into a girl who was drunk, stoned, and sleeping. He answered himself by turning off the dome light, starting the car, and taking her home. The denouement came when he helped her up the porch steps and to her front door and she giggled, "You missed your only chance, kiddo."

CHAPTER 4

Clive only came back to relatively full consciousness when he found himself next to an old crab apple tree in bloom near a large willow tree and a bog that was perhaps an acre in size with cattails, some uprooted by muskrats for food. The bog had once been a small pond beside a bone yard where milk cows that had died from natural causes or disease were dragged by harnessed Jerry or later on by the tractor. His immediate surroundings told Clive that he was at the back of the property due west of his mother's house. He could continue west and come out in an open field and take a circular route back home but it would be far longer and involve climbing a couple of fences, an irritation he wasn't ready for. There was an urge to find a grassy spot and take a nap but the air was full of those bloodsucking pests, mosquitoes, and he could only diminish the bites by keeping moving at a good

41

pace. Unfortunately the paths weren't laid out on a geometric grid but wandered left and right, and short of busting brush in dead reckoning he was trapped by the established route set by his mother and Margaret's sons and Sabrina who had come all the way from San Francisco to help out. Clive had never been a good navigator. Once in his early teens he had gone fishing with his father and they had walked a long path through the woods to a small lake where they kept a cheap aluminum rowboat. Clive had forgotten the can of worms in the pickup and when he fetched the can had strayed from the path back to the lake while looking at wildflowers. He heard his father calling and was finally able to thrash through the thick undergrowth to the lake.

His irritation was growing over his lack of mosquito repellent and the map, plus his expensive pair of Italian walking shoes were wet and muddy. He was also angry at Laurette's part in his indiscretion. As a northern Midwesterner, Clive overrated sincerity but Laurette had no compunctions about fibbing or outright lying. In their long childhood friendship he had been a quizzical, tolerant boy but by high school he had figured out that she was three girls in one. First of all she was his friend, second a member of the *in* crowd at school, and thirdly, she was a jittery waif with a largely absent father, no brothers and sisters, and a mother obsessed with her flower and vegetable gardens and English mysteries. When she was a kindergartner her parents had moved north from Grand Rapids where her father had a good job with a grocery store chain. Her father had a fantasy about becoming a farmer but was ill prepared for the relentless labor. Laurette's family were referred to as "new people" and would have been if they had lived in the locale fifty years. Her father had returned to his job in Grand Rapids promising to visit each weekend but gradually his trips back north became rare and local gossip had it that he had been seen with other women.

Clive was well into college before it occurred to him that naturally Laurette had chosen Keith and his family's big farm for reasons of stability and, of course, she blamed her mother for her father's disappearance. He questioned again on his path back through the thicket to Mother's house how memories could resume so much energy as if they were waiting in the landscape, waiting to attack. He rarely thought of Laurette in New York City except in erotic moments when the vision of her turning over on the car seat so he could see both sides continued to dumbfound him. On his obligatory trips back home she again returned vividly to the point that he would become exasperated. He had anyway forbidden Margaret to share any gossip with him, to which she had unsuitably replied, "No one gets over anything."

He was thinking of Jung's idea that perhaps dreams reside in the landscape. Children in Europe dream of knights in shining armor while American youngsters dream of wild animals. A doe and little fawn flushed in front of him and it dawned on him that he was facing the late afternoon sun, thus the path had looped and he was going away from home. He bellowed "fuck" in the loudest voice he remembered ever using. Within a minute or two he heard the dog whistle and plunged in a beeline straight for the house. Fortunately Margaret kept blowing the whistle every minute or two and he refused to acknowledge any diverting thought as the branches of bushes whipped at his face and body, and blackberry thorns tore one of his favorite linen shirts and trousers.

After a shower, a short nap, half a cup of coffee, and a very large martini made from a bottle in his luggage his brain stopped whirling and the anger from his misadventure subsided. His mother normally forbade hard liquor in her home, though wine and beer were okay, thinking of it as satanic fuel but having enough sense not to say anything noting that her son was past his wit's end. Her granddaughter had sent a case of wine from San Francisco two years before but she was saving the bottles for a special occasion that would likely never arrive.

At dinner Clive had become quite spooked because the memory of a dinner forty years before flooded the table. It had been spring of his sophomore year in college and Margaret had been fourteen. Their father had drowned two months before at the beginning of March. In the previous October his father had lost his right hand to a malfunctioning corn picker and had loathed his prosthetic device. His father had spent much of his last winter at solitary ice fishing on a nearby lake and the evening of his death he had driven his pickup out to his shanty and the ice had been weakened by a late February thaw. Clive privately thought of his father's death as a suicide because he had always been a cautious man. The consensus in the neighborhood was alcohol. It wasn't so rare that a vehicle had plunged through the ice after the driver had too much to drink and was too lazy to walk out to his ice shanty from the shore. Clive's father had been in the Orville tavern for a couple hours. Enough said.

Clive was remembering the dinner so long ago when his mother had angrily said that since Clive wouldn't quit college and come home and run the farm she would enroll at Central Michigan University in Mount Pleasant and take a teaching degree. The insurance company for the corn picker had made a modest but immediate settlement so she better figure out how to make a living. Mount Pleasant wasn't that far away and she would only be gone three nights a week. Margaret at fourteen was grown enough to take care of herself. His mother had finished her dinner speech by saying, "You've failed us, son."

The main reason Clive felt that suicide was probable was because on a car ride at Christmas on a snowy day his father had said, "If anything happens to me don't become a goddamn farmer. Stick to your art." His father had been a transport pilot during the Korean War and had wanted to become an airline pilot but instead had taken over the family farm after his own father had an early heart attack.

Now forty years later Margaret and his

mother were sitting at the same places at the old oak table in the kitchen and Clive was feeling a deep slippage in his life. Was Mother still saying "You've failed us, son" in her mind? He felt unconcerned but there was still an eerie sense that his mind had never quite admitted what happened to him in the ensuing time, which had become so palpable that he felt he could weigh time in his hand. The sense of slippage came from the sense that there was no traction for the future in his current life. Coming home he no longer had any belief in the life he had adopted after quitting painting. Twenty years had been lost in the cultural mists during which the world had become utterly usurious, drunk on the puke of its productions. It was so obvious in New York but he had seen it everywhere in his beloved Europe which, after all, was not a museum for aesthetes like himself. When he had quit painting he had lost his almost childish sense of destiny, which had been akin to the belief boys playing catch would generate that they would likely make the big leagues, the Detroit Tigers in fact.

"It would be nice if you'd paint the garage. It's not like the house which is high and dry. The back of the garage is in the shade and the boards are beginning to rot from moisture."

"Of course I will." He was wondering why an eighty-five-year-old woman would worry about garage boards rotting.

"Also the culvert under the driveway at the ditch needs to be cleaned out. It nearly flooded in April."

He nodded in assent watching Margaret's eyebrows lift in disbelief as she ate her unseasoned slice of pork roast. Mother had always believed that seasoning beyond salt and pepper was a sign of moral weakness. He was agreeable about painting the garage because he had a good memory about painting the granary at age twelve. It took a week but Dad had given him twenty bucks with which he bought his first oils. Up until then he had used pastels and caseins but the caseins were expensive which was how he had arrived at painting miniatures no larger than seven inches by nine. It was too expensive to work larger. The broad heavy strokes of painting the granary red were sheer pleasure. Margaret who was only a fourth grader had done the meticulous job of the two paned windows of the granary and the door in a flat white.

"Your hotshot girlfriend bought her old family home down the road." His mother laughed, awaiting his discomfort.

"That's nice," he said firmly to shut off the line of talk, then glancing at Margaret whom he had forbidden to ever mention Laurette's name. Margaret shrugged looking at a typed list of European recommendations Clive had made for her and which she wanted to discuss.

"She's not here very often. She has this little Cessna she flies up from Grand Rapids and then she keeps a yellow Jeep at the Reed City airport. A girlfriend lives in the house. She's a poet whatever that means these days. Of course there's been talk," Margaret said.

"I can't understand why anyone would want a yellow vehicle," his mother said huffily.

Clive was dealing with a mind full of bubbling distractions so he got up and went to the kitchen window above the sink. From his dinner seat, the view from the window had looked amazingly abstract in the way things can look if you're thinking about something else and not trying to make what you see cohere.

"There's a yellow bird in the willow outside the window," he remarked.

"A yellow-rumped warbler. She's nesting. Try not to bother her," his mother said matter-of-factly.

Margaret took her mother for an evening ride to look at all flying creatures and Clive made himself busy doing the dishes. The yellow-rumped warbler was sitting in her nest not ten feet away, undisturbed and looking at him, evidently used to someone through the window at the sink. He began to think about Laurette, with no discernible rise in blood pressure. He knew she had had a fifteen-year childless marriage to Keith and then had gone off to Grand Rapids to work for the same grocery chain as her father. Barren women had a difficult time in farm families. Keith had remarried and raised a satisfactory brood. That is all he knew about Laurette and he had no intention of asking Margaret for information. At the moment scouring the roast pork pan that could have used some garlic and fresh sage he was struggling for clarity that would dismiss the eerie feeling that had befallen him during dinner. He was thinking that principles were for academics. The working painter or even poet gets his hands dirty in the matter of the world. He, Clive, had become a foreman of sorts, a company stiff despite the power of his early idealism. During the twenty years since quitting painting he had prospered but not to the point he could afford a thirty-five-hundred-dollar-a-month apartment, five times the original rent in 1989. Were his twenty years *in the arts,* as it were, any different from Laurette hanging in there with a grocery chain? There was an obvious vulgarity to nearly all livelihoods that was disarming. Perhaps the percentage of trash in the art world was the same as that in supermarkets? He had been out in the parking lot playing air guitar. He hadn't made the cut.

He was outside in the twilight looking up at a gathering of stratocumulus clouds when Margaret and his mother came back from bird-watching. He was thinking that if he painted the whale skeleton, POV from the interior, he might add some distant clouds on the ceiling or was that too much? Laurette had certainly refused to pose nude but he had done a nice little painting of her back between waist and neck. He had long since recognized that most of his delusion about being a somewhat successful artist in his late twenties had come from his wife Tessa's money and their living in a nice apartment in SoHo with his studio down the hall.

His mother was effusively happy from seeing her first Virginia rail in a marsh down the road. He was uncomfortable at the memory of Sabrina when she was seven pointing out a rail in the same marsh so long ago. He said he saw it before he did and she had said, "You don't act like you see it," and then he did, with the rail's neck stretched straight upward looking something like a dead cattail.

His mother, as always, went to bed at nine with her ritual cup of hot cocoa, and he sat down with Margaret and her European list and they wrangled for an hour. She thought his choices in Paris and Florence too pricey. He said, "Be thrifty at home but splurge in Europe." She was going to be accompanied by a local schoolteacher, a friend since childhood, who had been saving for the trip for years.

"Just tell her I gave you money to upgrade the hotels." He wanted her to stay at the Hotel de Suède on rue Vaneau in Paris. It was a short walk to the Rodin Gardens, also the Jeu de Paume, or the d'Orsay Impressionist collection housed in an old railroad station, he forgot which. Of more interest to Margaret was the presence of the Bon Marché food court, a single long block from the hotel. You couldn't very well eat two full French meals a day and at Bon Marché you could buy limitless picnics to go. Like everyone else in the world she was worried about her digestion while traveling.

At dawn her mother was up packing ham

sandwiches and sniffling before her bird-watching.

"My baby is going across the ocean," she said.

Margaret and Clive were drinking weak coffee at the kitchen table wordlessly pondering the word *baby*. As long as you're around you're still her children. Margaret was fully dressed and packed two hours before departure, itching to get out of town.

PART II

CHAPTER 5

On a fine midmorning at the beginning of the second week of May Clive was feeling ordinary mostly because he was washing his mother's Camry, not as easy a job as he had expected. It had been forty years since he had washed a car and he had suggested that he drive the car to Reed City to a car wash. She thought that was wasteful what with gas at $2.89 a gallon. He was wearing his father's bib overalls and knee-high rubber boots he had found at the back of a capacious hall closet. There was certainly no reason to wear his own fine clothes in the area. He had noted when driving into Reed City or Big Rapids he was invisible in his dad's clothing. Just another farmer, like janitors are invisible in their green janitor suits.

He and Margaret and Sabrina had shared the cost of the new Camry two years before and had had it delivered. It was 6:30 a.m.

on a very hungover morning in New York when the thank-you call came. He was in bed with a ditz, a lingerie model to be exact, who had kept him awake until 3 a.m. talking about, among other things, her raw food diet with a trace of cocaine on her upper lip.

"Thank you, son, but I didn't need a radio."

"All cars come with radios," he croaked.

He heard the warbler in the willow and turned to look at it carefully. Early that morning on their bird walk he had proudly pointed to the yellow-rumped warbler at the back of the property in a Russian olive tree and had been embarrassed.

"Don't be stupid, son. That's a house finch. The yellow is much more intense. Can't you see?" she said squinting with her tunnel vision.

He had felt like he had mistaken a Giotto for a Schnabel. He had made a fair living out of the acuity of his vision and had stumbled over a bird weighing an ounce or so but then yellow had never been a persistent color for painters. While attempting to make the Camry windows streak-free he pondered yellow with momentary disgust thinking of the Art Tart throwing the paint on his precious suit, a suit that had drawn dozens of compliments in its lifetime. His irritation quickly bored him. After a quick peek the second day back on the farm he hadn't opened his laptop. Margaret was an addict and had had Wi-Fi set up but the wind of curiosity had gone out of him with the joking done in the spirit of schadenfreude by colleagues and acquaintances. A friend in Nîmes had sent an elaborate pun on the word *jaune* but the language was pitilessly complicated, and another in Siena had sent a photo of a big homely girl in a yellow dress. When he had received his first big box of crayons on his seventh Christmas he had been infatuated with colors and yellow had been one of his favorites. By wretched coincidence he heard a weak horn beep and there was Laurette in her open yellow Jeep at the foot of the driveway. There was an impulse to spray her with the hose but instead he walked down the driveway. Coming closer he noted that she looked fairly well with a few tiny wrinkles in the corners of her eyes and mouth, though it was immediately obvious that she had been redone.

"I've Googled you now and then Mister Bigshot," she said with a laugh. "Lately you've had some problems that they called an altercation."

"It will pass," he said wondering again how widely the most nominal news passes into the public. "You're looking good."

"It's hard work at my age. It even takes medical help." She turned her head slowly. "Can you tell?"

"No, not really. Maybe a slightly burnished patina on your left temple."

"Oh, screw you. It cost me fifteen grand. I showed the gals in the office your picture in *Newsweek.*"

It had been a small photo and item in the arts section. He had examined the collection of a kindly old woman in Texas and discovered three fakes including a Winslow Homer. It simply wasn't in Homer's palette to paint the picture. Her son, the usual weasel lawyer from Dallas, had tried to enjoin Clive from making any public comment about the collection, something he never would have done anyway but then the man in threatening tones tried to get him to verify the painting before an upcoming auction, so Clive went public with Liz Smith, whom he had met at a number of parties.

"Come over at six for a drink." Laurette's cell phone rang. He heard her say, "Tell that asshole that we won't take any more of his smoked pork products." She turned off the phone. "Come over at six for a drink," she

60

repeated.

"I shouldn't leave Mother."

"Oh nonsense. Margaret leaves her all the time to see her boyfriend up in Manton. Besides she lived alone for forty years. Also she has a twenty-two rifle with which she shoots stray cats that are after her birds. I heard shooting and asked her about it at the grocery store."

Laurette spun off throwing gravel and Clive reflected on how women could shut you out. Margaret never mentioned a boyfriend up in Manton. Mother with a rifle? Probably his boyhood Remington .22 single shot. Laurette hadn't waited to hear if he was coming for a drink or not.

In another half hour of touching up he was absurdly proud of the gleaming Camry. Another career opportunity in a glum economy, he joked to himself. In the morning he had to drive her to Big Rapids to church and she'd probably tell her friends, "My son the art bigwig washed my car." The first Sunday he had insisted on sitting out in the car, which had made her angry so that she extracted a promise to attend beside her. There was a bit of dread attached to the promise. He smiled at the memory of his wife Tessa saying after she had first met his mother, "She's a real hard-ass. I'm surprised you're not more fucked-up than you are." As a rich girl from an Episcopalian family in Pasadena, Tessa loved to swear.

He went in, cleaned up, and had a small glass of Côtes du Rhône he had managed to find in a supermarket. His mother was preparing supper, dicing up the leftover pork roast and the potatoes, onions, and carrots that had cooked with it into a hash, which was one of the few dishes from the Midwest he missed. He told her he was going over to have a drink with Laurette.

"It's your funeral, son." The evident anguish Laurette had put her son through in high school was still unforgivable. And how could she have divorced Keith and given up on the best farm in the county? Teaching had been a livelihood but a farm was a life.

CHAPTER 6

It was a mental funeral. The interior of Laurette's old stone farmhouse was startling with too much white everywhere on the walls and carpet and that outré blond furniture called Danish modern. There were several gauche bullfight posters from Seville and Granada that Clive perceived to be genuine rather than riffraff reproductions. Laurette's house sitter or whatever met him at the door and introduced herself as Lydia. She was handsome, pouty, and bored in a short green skirt and white sleeveless blouse. She said that Laurette was in the shower and pointed to the side table with bottles and ice. He could hear a hair dryer down the hall above an annoyingly emotional CD of Mendelssohn that jarred him.

"Lydia? That's a rare name these days."

"It's my nom de plume. I'm a poet. It's just Lydia. No last name."

She plopped herself down on the sofa

showing a good deal of leg which Clive thought she perceived as her best feature. Her head struck him as a tad small and her black hair had small empire curls at the temple like the old pictures of Emily Brontë and Emily Dickinson.

"You like it here?" Clive had made himself an overfull drink to melt the awkward ice in the room. He noted a platter of carrot and celery sticks surrounding a cup of dip on the coffee table, also the cheddar cubes and ripe olives that went with cocktails in the northern Midwest where the quasi food revolution was not apparent.

"I love it here. I'm from Chicago. There's no nature there. Laurette is giving me space to find my voice as a poet."

The language made his jaw ache. Previously when he had come home for a visit he hadn't come home in spirit, but now the whole of him was stuck there. Why did so many young people want to become painters, poets, environmentalists, or chefs? How ill-advised. He wondered what was wrong with engineering, though aside from trains he had no idea what engineers did. In New York window washing was the most daring job. Window washers were jaunty and women adored them high up there working away so we could see clearly. He drank deeply and glanced up Lydia's green skirt, well up in fact. The legs were tan from the South or a tanning parlor. Lydia aimed a clicker at the CD player and the music segued to Brahms, another of Clive's hundreds of bêtes noires.

"Brahms mellows me," Lydia offered.

"Why not roll in a tub full of warm butter," Clive joked and she giggled and gave him the finger which he thought charming. He got up and made an equally large second drink. He felt a specific dislocation looking out the south window because the barn door in the distance was still off its hinges and the silo was in the same state of disrepair as forty years before.

"I'm smoking a joint because my favorite gin adds pounds to my ass," said Laurette entering the room in soft mannish slacks and a peach-colored short-sleeve sweater. "Talk about six degrees of separation, which no one was. I forgot to tell you that a friend in San Francisco went to a party at your ex-wife's lavish home. You lost a gold mine. She's living with a young man half her age, lucky girl. We have to leave for a dinner in half an hour. You could tag along but you have to look after your mother. When it warms up we'll have to go skinny-dipping at the lake like we used to." She passed the joint to Lydia who demurred.

"I'm the designated driver. Remember?"

"Of course, dear."

Laurette rattled on but Clive wasn't listening to the particulars. She certainly looked ten years younger than her sixty. Many women kept themselves so well these days compared to the men. He had seen a big man jogging behind the Metropolitan Museum one Saturday stop at a vendor's for two hot dogs with kraut and then a leisurely cigarette. He had certainly never been skinny-dipping with Laurette and the *in* crowd. "Remember our last night in the car before I got married to Keith? Afterward I was worried that I might be pregnant." She laughed.

"We never closed the deal," Clive said in a semihuff.

Suddenly Lydia lunged forward, grabbed the appetizer platter, and threw it high toward Clive. In a millisecond he thought, *What the fuck, has she gone mad?* and ducked. The celery and carrot sticks, olives and cheese cubes, cup of dip were realistically made of plastic and the platter clattered to the floor intact.

"It's an objet d'art," Laurette shrieked, laughing while Lydia settled for smirking. Laurette pronounced *objet* as in *jet* plane.

It went poorly after the flying appetizers. They were no match for Clive's talents at Manhattan condescension.

"It's interesting to see what happens to art when it works its way down the food chain," Clive said, composing himself.

"What do you mean?" they asked in unison.

"I mean that historically art doesn't necessarily include needlepoint hot pads and macramé plant hangers. Eisenhower painted well by numbers, and Charlotte Moorman did OK playing the cello in the nude. Hobbyism therapy is quickly yesterday's pizza. Trying to teach creativity is the major hoax of our time along with the Iraq war and plastic surgery."

"What a fucking prick you are. A prick and a prig. It was just a joke," Lydia huffed.

Laurette bounced off the couch and jumped very high, quite stoned. "I don't know much but I know what I think," she said in a parody of a widespread attitude.

"She works out on a minitrampoline. It's a new thing," Lydia said in response to Clive's raised eyebrows. She gave him one more good peek up her green skirt. It was girlish but fun. In her poems she did not avoid the merging of organs. At the workshops at Carnegie Mellon University in

Pittsburgh she had the pleasure of noting the unrest of the young males when she read aloud her dampish sexual poems.

On the short drive home his brain was antic enough from two large drinks to enjoy the trivialization of everything including himself.

He swerved to avoid a rabbit and came altogether too close to the deep ditch which was momentarily sobering. As a boy he would shoot and clean rabbits and his dad would fry them. They both loved rabbit and venison. His father shot a deer every late fall but his mother wouldn't eat wild game which didn't lessen the pleasure taken in it by her husband and son. She would eat a bowl of barley soup in the parlor because of her intense empathy with the natural world, which did not include the human species except blacks and Indians.

In the driveway he got out of the car too quickly and felt dizzy so he put a hand against the rough bark of a maple tree to steady himself. He was suddenly quite tired of the mythology he had constructed for his life. The idea of having quit painting was far too neat. He had lost heart, run out his string, or the homely idea he had painted himself into a small dark corner. Back then there were hundreds of artists in the city trying to attract Leo Castelli and other prominent gallery owners who were clearly unable to democratically sort out the good and the bad in the hordes. Much later he figured it had been like Hollywood trying to predict a trend. The dominant problem, however, on a day-to-day basis had been Tessa's burgeoning obsession with Tibetan Buddhism. For a number of years their frequent parties in the loft had been fun and then suddenly the parties were too full of these people eating yogurt and *tsampa* and drinking tea with yak butter which was expensive and hard to get but Tessa managed. They were a bit scruffy like folk music people used to be and left out indefinite articles in a faux Oriental patois. He couldn't comprehend these Tibetan Buddhists any more than he could all the varieties of Protestantism. The true beginning of the end came when he refused to accompany Tessa on what she called a "pilgrimage" to Kathmandu one August. She also intended to visit the Bodhi Tree in India where the Buddha had achieved what Tessa referred to as "perfect realization." Summertime in India? I think not. She had also insisted on taking along little Sabrina who was five at the time. He feared his daughter catching a disease and sure enough Sabrina had had to be hospitalized for dysentery in Calcutta which he had imagined to be chock full of snake charmers and starving riffraff in dirty turbans.

He looked straight up at a raucous blackbird scolding him. He still felt a bit dizzy and wondered idly if it were something more than the alcohol. Perhaps a coronary? He unwittingly pulled away the hand braced against the maple trunk to feel his chest and pitched sideways to the ground. No real damage was done except a loss of wind, though his head had narrowly missed one of the railroad ties that lined the driveway. He didn't stop thinking, and immediately ascribed the fall to a freshly learned concept of impermanence but then the question quickly arose of why everything he does should be of importance as if it were being written in a story? Had even his love for Tessa with her high Botticelli forehead come from an art book? The point of view was interesting, looking straight up at the silvery undersides of the maple leaves. Suddenly his mother wordlessly appeared above him and poured a pitcher of water down onto his upturned face. His scrambled brain slowed the course of the water. His dad had said that Ted Williams could see the seam of a baseball pitched at 100 mph. She helped him into the house, through the kitchen to the stairs to the second story. Still a tad dizzy he half crawled upward, hearing her slam the stairwell door behind him.

CHAPTER 7

He awoke at midnight according to his cell phone which wouldn't work out here in the country. He had a headache, a pointless hard-on, and was sweaty from sleeping in his clothes. He was also very hungry and a suppressed memory had arisen from when Laurette had shown him out the door and had whispered with a glance at Lydia in the yard, "I drive both ways on the freeway," meaning, he suspected, that she and Lydia slept together however crude the expression. On the way out Laurette's driveway he had paused to watch Lydia in Laurette's ancient tire swing pumping ever higher and offering him a lavish display of the undersides of her thighs up to her black panties. Maybe the rope will break, he had thought.

He tried to dispel the overgenerous sequence of nightmares during his five-hour nap by staring out the window at a three-quarter moon rising through the top of the willow so that the tree's branches looked almost flossy. He tried to think about how our vision tends to be partial and semi-abstract when you stop the brain from making sense from it. That didn't work. Unlike Tessa who had gone through Jungian dream therapy at enormous cost, Clive put no stock in his dream life. Her endless banal recitation of her dream life had made him irritable. Where's the story in the story? His nightmare had been long-winded and tedious and was comprised of his gay, meticulous art history professor showing an endless five-hour display of slides of colors. No objects, just gradations of colors, variations of the primaries. In the nightmare Clive was aware of clutching his Christmas gift box of seventy crayons. His heart and head ached from the thousands of slides.

Hunger brought him back to full consciousness, also the memory of his only truly positive sexual experience in New York. It happened about five years before when he was in his midfifties. She was a waitress in a simple Greek diner way over in the midfifties. She was in her midtwenties, from Fort Wayne, Indiana, and trying to be an actress of course. He was given to taking very early and very long walks on the West Side to keep his body from deliquescing at a faster rate than it already was. After a half dozen visits to the diner they were nearly friends. She had a single art history course at the University of Indiana and claimed to be a distant relative of the painter Sheeler. She said that he was the first man she had ever met who knew who Sheeler was. He took her out to Babbo and Del Posto, restaurants she could never afford and he could only barely. Her name was odd, Kara, and her body was undramatically perfect, the divine ordinary. They made love only three times before she announced she was returning to Indiana to marry her home-town lover, Josh. The last time he had awakened at four in the morning without her in bed and found her in his study look-ing through a pile of art books in the nude. They had made love against the desk and it had been the most convulsive orgasm he had had since parting from Tessa fifteen years before. They had gone to Barney Greengrass for breakfast and he had never seen a woman eat so much herring for breakfast. It amazed him, but then she dis-appeared and he never saw or heard from her again. New York was like that but he still thought of her frequently. He had taken her to a Joshua Bell concert and she had wept profusely at the beauty of the music.

He made his way quietly downstairs and heated up the roast pork hash noting that Mother had eaten more than her share. He chuckled at his foolishness in drinking two large glasses of vodka on an empty stomach at his age. Some fool had written about a man's sixties being the new fifties which he certainly didn't believe. He imagined geezers wandering around with knapsacks laden with Viagra. He got out his laptop ignoring thirty-seven e-mails, found a site, and ordered a deluxe box of crayons to be FedExed overnight. Now that he was on a roll he also made a big order from Zingerman's deli in Ann Arbor. He had nearly three weeks to go on his mother-sitting and couldn't envision enduring the purgatory of her bland cooking. He chuckled again imagining Laurette driving on a freeway in her yellow Jeep with both male and female sexual partners.

"Please go to bed, son, you're keeping me awake." His mother peeked from her bedroom door.

Back upstairs he kept his night-light on for fear that the nightmare might return. It had been his first in recent memory. There had been a poignant mudbath in the loft so many years before, when Tessa and her friends had done Tibetan chants all night for a mutual friend who had died of breast cancer. He couldn't very well object. Tessa had remodeled a small guest bedroom toward the back of the loft and had decorated it just so with Oriental bric-a-brac. He couldn't stand earplugs but while sleeping intermittently he had dreamt of being trapped in the middle of a herd of elephants. In the nightmare he was also hearing Mozart's "Grand Partita" but the music was horribly distorted. It was a curious relief when the elephants trampled him into a bloody pancake.

He glanced over at the bookcase, dismissing the idea of rereading *The Moon and Sixpence,* a fictionalized rendering of the life of Gauguin. There were others that had poisoned his teens with their romanticism, including novels on the lives of van Gogh, Toulouse-Lautrec, Modigliani, and Caravaggio. At sixteen he had wept until his pillow was wet over the murder of Caravaggio. There were also dreary texts by Berenson, Herbert Read, and a tome by Gombrich.

He suddenly wished he had a photo of Kara from Indiana to put on the wall. There was the abrupt idea that he could easily paint her likeness from memory. He closed his eyes and could see her perfectly. Who would care? No one of course. He had anyway exhausted his feeling of failure over quitting painting twenty years before. The only remnant of the guilt came from having failed his father, a residual nexus of emotions from his father being proud that his son would be an artist rather than a farmer. He mentally organized a self-mocking headline "Professor Takes Up Painting Again" but the irony, as always, was weak-kneed, wobbly in fact. He wanted to see Kara again so he could paint her alive. Simple enough. There was immense freedom in not having a career to protect. His mind, a virtual encyclopedia of the history of art, briefly whirled with likes and dislikes. He never cared for Warhol, Johns, Rauschenberg, or Judy Chicago. He rather liked Franz Kline, Motherwell, Helen Frankenthaler, and the long forgotten Abe Rattner and Syd Solomon, and even the more recent Ed Ruscha. But he loved Burchfield and Walter Inglis Anderson not to speak of Edward Hopper. He lay there feeling pleasantly irrelevant, recalling a Toronto periodical called *Brick* that a friend had given him, in which there was a goofy essay about food that included a comment to the effect that 99.999 percent of all writers, poets, painters, sculptors, and composers are eliminated in their last act and once you reach sixty you had to kill your ego so that you wouldn't become desperately unhappy about disappearing in your old age. It wasn't up to you anyway. Your life's work would become a mild quarrel among the air guitarists.

Turning in the bed he could see Henry Miller's *To Paint Is to Love Again* beneath a slender folio of Pascin. His daughter Sabrina had given him the book when she was twelve and feeling insufficiently loved. He liked Miller's work very much but had never opened the book under the notion that he didn't want to be disappointed with the man's views on painting. He had seen a few of Miller's aquarelles in the possession of a collector in L.A. and they were almost nice though the painter was trying something beyond his capabilities. These thoughts made him feel priggish. Miller had seemed quite happy in his last decade unlike most artists. He painted, played a lot of Ping-Pong, and was involved with younger women. This reminded Clive of Goethe who at seventy-three had gone into a depression because the eighteen-year-old girl next door wouldn't marry him. This was an amusing presumption by a mountainous ego.

Clive dozed for a few moments then awoke to a moth battering itself against the bed lamp. How could he paint Kara without supplies? He got up and rummaged at the back of his big closet. Luckily his mother never threw anything away and he found a set of caked and cracked watercolors that could be revived, but the tubes of oil were all toast except unopened tubes of Titanium White and Burnt Umber. There was also his flimsy twelve-dollar easel from his twelfth Christmas. He would get on the laptop and order some minimal supplies. He knew that in the back of the garage in his father's huge tool chest there was still a stack of seven-inch-by-nine-inch pieces of Masonite that had been cut for his early efforts. With an undercoat of white they would suffice. He smiled remembering again the blimpish matron who popped out the paintings at the fair saying that she only wanted the frames. He knew that he was going to feel awful in the morning, both fatigued and enervated, but so what? He used to paint up to eighteen hours a day in a frenzy and Tessa would bring a liquid health food concoction to give him energy which he often dumped out a window in his studio into the alley below. He doubted that even rats would find the combination of the blender-whipped carrot, beet, and bananas palatable. He thought that discomfort might be new and interesting in that he had so studiously avoided it in recent years with his two short naps per day, a modest walk, and good meals. The closest he came to discomfort was jet lag, but on his morning arrivals in Spain, France, and Italy he would loll around the first day before the somewhat busy schedule of the second, and in recent years he had been uniformly successful in wheedling a business class seat from his hosts.

He recalled cutting wood with his father. A neighbor a mile away had timbered his woodlot but there were many huge branches of beech, oak, and maple, all marvelous firewood. They had worked through an afternoon that featured high winds and an ice storm in late October. Passage through the woods and fallen branches was tight so they had brought Jerry dragging the stone boat rather than the tractor and wagon. By the time that they had cut three cords their coats were crunchy with ice. Wheat and corn prices were real low that fall and all of this work was to save buying fifty bucks' worth of firewood. Besides, it was frowned on to buy wood when you should be cutting it yourself unless you were infirm. They reached home just before dark, fed Jerry and rubbed him down, and finally in the house shedding their wet clothes before the hot bellied stove his father had poured them each a couple of ounces of cheap whiskey to the disapproval of his mother. They ate pot roast and gravy with a mixture of whipped potatoes and rutabaga and boiled cabbage, all with his mother's tart corn relish. He had gone to bed at eight but it was midnight before he was truly warm. He had neglected his homework but he got straight As and could fake it. He had risen early the next morning and had begun a painting of Jerry's huge body steaming from exertion on the way home in the ice storm.

CHAPTER 8

Behind the wheel while driving to church he began to nod a bit which his mother noticed and insisted he pull over so she could drive the dozen miles, always harrowing as she drove fast right down the middle of the road. He felt none too well but better than expected. He had stayed out at dawn with Mother at station no. 5 in the thicket. He would never enter the thicket again without Margaret's map. She had trilled happily at hearing a number of species, especially three new spring warblers, one he thought to be absurdly colored orange and black called Blackburnian. They had had the unvarying Sunday breakfast of thick bacon, eggs, and fried slices of cornmeal mush with local maple syrup. He had once told her that in the outside world cornmeal mush was called polenta. "I call it cornmeal mush," she had said, plainly not interested. After breakfast he had ordered art supplies on his laptop and was startled when she said that Margaret had told her that even women watched pornography on their computers.

"That's what the world has come to," she said washing the breakfast dishes. She suddenly laughed saying that she knew her father had always had a calendar of naked ladies out in the barn. This was untypical indeed as she never spoke about sex. He wished the barn was still there as he could have set up a studio in the mow. She had sold the barn thirty years before to a company that dealt in barn wood and beams for remodels with a country touch.

He drove poorly on the way to church because of drowsiness and paying too much attention to herds of milk cows and the burgeoning number of saddle horses boarded on farms by the town dwellers in Reed City and Big Rapids. He had read in the *Times* that this spike in saddle horse ownership had slowed precipitously but here plain as day in northern Michigan was an imitation Kentucky horse farm with white wooden fences. His mother was in a snit about his wobbly driving and had him stop so she could drive. When he got out of the car and crossed the ditch to get a close look at a group of horses she yelled out, "Come back, son, we'll be late for church!"

He had observed these horses several times on the way to town for groceries since Margaret had left nine days before. On one side of the fence there were two horses, a white and a bay, and on the other side there were seven horses. They were staring at each other from approximately the same positions each time he passed.

"What's going on here? Do horses communicate?" he asked getting in the passenger side of the car.

"Of course," she said, speeding off. "All creature species talk to each other. Mice do choral singing and many birds use hundreds of different songs. You should try reading something outside of art books."

He let this pass. He had recently been trying to read a short volume called *The Mapmaker's Dream* about early Renaissance perceptions on how the world is shaped. The narrator was a monk in Venice who never went anyplace and depended on the testimonies of early world travelers who passed through the waterlogged city. Clive had always felt claustrophobic at the Venice Biennale even in the old days in Peggy Guggenheim's huge apartment. In the book each location tried to exclude the reality of other locations, an agreeable notion as Clive had observed that the Hudson and East

River in New York were walls that held out the rest of the world. A very old man aged ninety-two in a neighboring apartment had given Clive the book. The man had been a prominent art history professor from a Midwestern university who had retired to the city to be close to museums. "I'm totally free. Everyone thinks I'm dead," the man had said merrily. They occasionally cooked lunch for each other and the ancient man was an excellent cook besides being the merriest soul Clive had ever met.

As they pulled up to the church Clive was still thinking about the shape of the world. Tens of thousands of painters and writers had seen the world differently and here he was, in front of the inscrutable church in an alien territory. Mother had decided he shouldn't attend because he might fall asleep, start snoring, and embarrass her. He was told to be back in an hour and drove a few blocks down to a small park on a high bank above the Muskegon River. It was a favorite place on trips to town in his child-hood when the park seemed hundreds of feet above the river and he judged now that his park bench was perhaps seventy feet up the bank. The world had clearly changed its shape. Nothing could be depended on. Usually his visits home had been three or four days at most and now this extended time made him feel tremulous. It was more than the feeling gotten on a ten-day trip to Paris when you tended to forget all about New York and when you returned the city would look a bit dowdy and strange. The present emotions were far more radical. His dad had always advised him to run a tight ship but this military metaphor was as irrelevant as the battle against cancer. He had always been scornful about the silly psychologisms surrounding the ubiquitous "midlife crisis" which seemed to ignore a late-life crisis. What was the shape of his own personal world? Perhaps time was clay that could be shaped and reshaped. It may have been that the wrong foot he had started on had been the refusal to accept the limits of his talents. His ambition as a teen to be a great painter was unlimited but then who could weigh the talent? Was the ambition to be an artist or to have a meteoric career as an artist, two quite different things? A pretty girl in shorts sped by on a bicycle altogether too fast giving him a fleeting glance at her admirable bottom and offering him the idea that he could paint Laurette nude from the waist down under the dome light of an old car.

He dozed waking ten minutes after he

should have picked up his mother. He
didn't bother rushing knowing that her
anger wouldn't depend on elapsed time but
the very fact that he was late at all. He had
the happy thought that he had zero percent
financing on the rest of his life because no
one more than nominally cared except
himself. He might be going mad as a hatter
but it hadn't been all that bad so far.

CHAPTER 9

It turned out that his mother was well toward the back of the churchyard under an ash tree and was effusively happy because she had heard her first oriole of the spring. He didn't want to beep the horn out on the street so he had walked back to where she stood oblivious to everything but the oriole up near the top of the budding ash tree. Margaret had said that mother could identify a couple hundred species by their songs. Was this possible? Why not?

On the drive home she had babbled on about the fact that a bird called the bar-tailed godwit migrated all the way from the Aleutians to New Zealand in nine days without stopping for a rest. This seemed improbable to him but she had gone on in detail about how the bird gorged on crustaceans until it was obese and could barely fly before it caught a big north wind and headed south on its ten-thousand-mile flight. The immutable specifics of the sciences had always made Clive feel a tad flimsy. He recalled a line of Wallace Stevens from a college American literature course to the effect that the worst of all things was not to live in a physical world. This segued to the notion that maybe if he were collapsing mentally it might be better to do it out in the country than in New York where so much of the physical world was comprised of cement. When he and Tessa had split up he had to spend much of the day walking or he was sleepless and these walks had to be along the East or Hudson rivers because there was something consoling about moving water that he couldn't identify.

On the outskirts of Big Rapids the girl he had seen near the river whizzed past through a stop sign and he admired again the flex of her fanny. Should he be beyond such voyeurism? If so what was beyond but further desuetude?

He came back to full consciousness from his butt reverie when his mother gestured at Ralph's, a small country grocer and gas station.

"It's not self-service. Ralph still pumps your gas and he's two years older than me."

She went into the store with an alacrity that surprised him. He was puzzled about her world, wherein a single oriole could cause a positive mood swing. He began thinking about a large can of oil-based white paint that Margaret had left in the garage, which she had used to paint a door in her bedroom. The paint would work fine as an undercoat for a dozen pieces of the humble Masonite. He liked the idea of starting small. The mechanics were easy in that once you learn to ride a bicycle skillfully you don't forget. Someone had said that "technique is the proof of your seriousness" but then of what worth is it, finally, if you are not engaged in what you are seeing? He knew a stylistically exquisite writer who did well but readily admitted that he had nothing whatsoever to say. Clive had taken pleasure in not really keeping up with the contemporary scene since he himself had quit. Besides, when he was evaluating a collection there was rarely anything new for major spenders, except maybe a stray Ed Ruscha now worth a million bucks. Sitting there in the vacant parking lot of Ralph's he wondered if Mike Ovitz still owned all of those Schnabels. Of course most art was finally discarded. Where were the millions of dollars Lucille Ball spent on sad-eyed clowns painted by Keane? He recalled a ten-by-twelve-foot abstract he had done that was painfully a derivative of de Kooning. Tessa had put all of his work in storage when he had escaped to Modena in Italy. He thought that the storage bill likely far exceeded the worth of the paintings.

His mother came out of Ralph's holding something behind her back with a mischievous smile. She came around to the driver's seat where he was hanging half out the window smoking a cigarette that was verboten in her car.

"Smell it. You loved it so as a child."

He smelled the brown paper wrapper. It was Ralph's homemade pickled bologna, scarcely Proust's madeleine but then he was scarcely Proust. The odor of this childhood treat swept him precipitously back to his childhood, sitting in the rowboat fishing for bluegills with his dad and eating sharp cheddar and pickled bologna with saltines.

"Thank you," he said with untypically complete sincerity.

When they got home his mother noted a phone message and answered a call from Sabrina in California. He didn't want to overhear the call and went back outside with a lump in his throat. How could he have let things degenerate so long with his only child? Three years before he had said something snide about Tessa's newest husband because he had imagined them living luxuriously while he, Clive, struggled with rising rent. Well, not quite *struggled* as that only befits ordinary people in the current economy, while he spent so much time around truly rich collectors that he was susceptible to feeling poor in comparison to their often absurd extravagances. He occasionally wished he were a poet as the poets he knew could babble elegantly on their feet. True, he wrote well but that was sheer hard labor. Most often while talking to people he tended to be brief, sardonic, laconic, as if he were learning to shuffle cards. Painters talked like that partly because they had spent so much time looking at the shape and color of their surroundings. For instance, right now from the patio, a yellow bird seemed trapped and lost within a thickish rosebush and the tininess of its body made him incapable of saying anything lucid.

"She sends her love to you. It's shameful you two don't resolve your quarrel. You're not going to live forever, Mister Bigshot," his mother said coming out to the patio.

CHAPTER 10

Early the next morning he painted white a dozen rectangles of Masonite in his room, and not wanting insects to stick to the surface, impatient for them to dry, he set up a floor fan. In the middle of the night he had slipped quietly downstairs for his laptop and, as an afterthought, his pickled bologna from the refrigerator. Mother had made fried chicken, the traditional after-church lunch, but then only a bowl of pea soup for supper. His Manhattan digestive system was geared to a bigger late dinner to put him to sleep until morning. What was in the pea soup? Dried peas. That's it folks. It cried out for a ham hock or a butt end of prosciutto.

He composed a long e-mail of apology to Sabrina, then with the aid of a bottle of Absolut vodka he had hidden in the closet, he reduced the verbose apology to a single reasonably lucid short paragraph. Why run on at the mouth?

Dearest Daughter,
    I want to apologize for my bad behavior a couple of years ago during dinner at Babbo. It was hideous for me to say those things about your mother and her new husband. It was none of my business. I have no excuse except that I was sort of broke at the time, also depressed. Please forgive me. Love, Dad.

He had sent it because it was only mid-evening in California what with the time change. He was sitting awkwardly at a school desk that was not nearly big enough. His father had bought the desk for three bucks when the country school down the road had closed. A bigger desk was in order, perhaps from a yard sale. He wished he had brought up some saltines to go with the pickled bologna and vodka. If only his gourmet group, a little club of three women and three men who cooked together once a month in the Village, could see him now. He would have to tell them as a poor farm boy his roots were in baloney and the baloney he had tried in Bologna was inferior to the Ralph's he was eating now. He reflected that in his twin career in the arts and academia there was a tendency to take everything you said and did far too seriously. Eating baloney after midnight was simply eating baloney after midnight. He recalled that when a friend at Gagosian had sent over a Richard Phillips catalog he had laughed aloud at a painting, a back view of a girl bending over in the nude, what the English would call a "fetching lass." He hoped his painting of Laurette on the car seat would be as erotic. The important thing was not to take himself too seriously. He had nearly three weeks of looking after his mother to go and painting could be construed as killing time. He would be a sixty-year-old Sunday painter painting every day. An everyday Sunday painter had a nice feeling to it.

In the morning when he finished the white undercoat he had the nice feeling of a little light being allowed to peek into his beleaguered soul. He recognized this as non-unique and probably shared by gardeners after finishing a row of weeding. In his case the good feeling was aided by Sabrina's e-mail response.

Dear Dad,
    All is forgiven. Let's get together ASAP. I would come out there for a few

days. I need a break from writing my dissertation. If you need money I have lots in trust from Grandpa's death. It started in New England in the 1700s from the spice and slave trade — amazing. Of course Mom's fourth marriage went kerplunk, another gold digger. She's at a Zen retreat, the same monastery Leonard Cohen goes to. She always loved his music. Did you know that song preceded language? See you soon.

Love, Saab

Her nickname had always been Saab like the car. He wished that he hadn't said that he was broke. Between his academic chair and his art sidelines he averaged about two hundred grand, certainly not all that much in Manhattan but nothing to whine about given the state of the national economy. Of course he had spent every cent he had ever made. Being married to Tessa for fifteen years hadn't been a good training ground. Even the well-off like to complain subtly to the very rich.

Suddenly he was preoccupied with the idea that song or music came before language. He had visited Lascaux in Dordogne several times, also Altamira in Spain. He tried to imagine primitive men singing as they painted before they had a defined language. Maybe they sang scatting like the jazz singer Annie Ross, harmonic nonsense syllables. They probably sang because they loved what they were doing.

His mother called up the stairs reminding him that he had promised her a rowboat ride to look at a heron rookery. That was fine as he couldn't very well sit there watching paint dry. He was also absurdly restive and eager for FedEx to arrive with his big box of Crayolas, his hundred-dollar kit of oil paints, and his food from Zingerman's.

It was a short drive to the small lake with several abrupt stops on the roadside for a look at one bird or another that his mother had heard in transit. She certainly had sharp ears for an oldster though her targets were singular. This made him think of his own intermittent acuity of vision. On his dozens and dozens of trips to the Metropolitan Museum, MoMA, the Frick, the Guggenheim and Whitney, his vision depended on the day, in short, his own peculiar state of mind. On the best visits certain paintings and parts of paintings became a permanent fixture in his neural structure so that they could be recalled in a split second at will. He suspected his mother's bird memories to be similar. Now passing a row of dilapidated fence posts he recalled that this was the location where she had pointed out a group of bluebirds more than forty years before. Memories reside in the landscape and arise when you revisit an area. If he could find his old car Laurette would still be nude on the front seat.

The farmer that owned the small private lake was stooped and thin, obviously arthritic, but insisted on carrying the wooden oars from a shed out to the lake about a hundred yards behind the barn. The farmer called Clive's mother "Coochie," evidently a nickname from over seventy years before. They were young once, Clive thought stupidly. The farmer shooed away a large coiled water snake near the bow of the boat. Clive helped his mother in and they were off across the lake with Clive enjoying the strain of rowing the heavy old boat.

He thought later that it was the metronomic physicality of rowing that reminded him of the graduality of his collapse, but the collapse was too dramatic a word for the snail's pace loss of cohesion. There's a comfort level for mental stability and falling a millimeter below this level could be unnerving indeed. There was a tinge of a vacuum beneath the breastbone and between the ears, and occasional spates of anger over meaningless matters like the horrors of airports that he normally endured stoically by reading Donna Leon or those lugubrious Scandinavian mysteries wherein the hero always has a cold and eats crummy food and drinks bad coffee. Quite abruptly the osso bucco and risotto Milanese he cooked for the food club didn't taste nearly as good.

Around the time of his quarrel with Sabrina nearly three years before he had flown to Minneapolis to give his patented speech "The Cost of Creation" at the Walker. According to his travel journal it was the eighth time he had offered this lecture on church and noble patronage as the sole livelihood for artists during the *Renascimento,* therefore his discourse was becoming tiresome. He had noticed an extremely vexed elderly lady in the second row seated next to her dozing husband. Usually he requested that questions for the necessary Q & A session be delivered to him on three-by-five cards to avoid long-winded people but had forgotten to mention this stricture to his hosts. The elderly woman had become any lecturer's nightmare. She had gotten up and faced the audience and rattled on about having lived in Italy for five years with her "important businessman" husband. She was clearly deranged and claimed to have visited every museum in Italy and had learned that all of the masterpieces were painted by "holy artists" purely out of love and it was hideous for Clive to put a money tag on their work. There was amused tittering in the audience as Clive ran his hands through his hair preparing an answer. As a New Yorker he wanted to go for the throat but started politely by saying that in Spain Goya had fathered nineteen children and they had required food and diapers so he had needed a paycheck, neglecting to mention that all but one had died.

"We're talking about Italy, Mister Big-shot."

It had amused him that she had used his mother's language but wanted very much to rid himself of this noxiousness so he said that just because a person lived in North Dakota didn't mean that they knew everything about American art. It was a low blow but well deserved. He went on to other questions but felt inexplicably enervated by this nitwit. He noticed the woman was weeping into her hands and afterward in the crowded lobby her husband had hissed at him, "You made my wife cry you New York faggot." Security had ushered the couple out but at a later dinner for the select he had become a little drunk and irascible. At dawn on the way to the airport he began to see his success in the arts as possibly a form of mental illness.

On the lake his mother had cooed and chuckled over the heron rookery and Clive had become as calm as the water except for wondering about his FedEx shipment. When he drove them into the driveway he could see the packages stacked against the kitchen door and his heart actually leapt. He spread his booty on the kitchen table, first opening the Zingerman's package as the contents would need to be refrigerated. He sniffed at the prosciutto, mortadella, *soppressata,* imported provolone, cream cheese for the dozen true bagels, the five French cheeses, and a full pound of belly lox. His mother tried to grab the enclosed bill for inspection but he beat her to it, an open act of rebellion, and she huffed off for a nap.

The twenty-four oils were fine though the tubes were smaller than in the old days and the sketch pads were thinner. He spent a full half hour on the deluxe package of 120 Crayolas, a bit expensive but the variety excited him. He was relieved that Raw Sienna and Burnt Umber and Forest Green were still there, but irked that Maize and

Violet Blue were gone, the latter the color of a winter twilight. Mulberry was also gone to the grave of dead Crayolas. He was also irritated that in 1993 consumers had been allowed to name new colors such as Razzmatazz, Asparagus, Macaroni and Cheese, and Timberwolf. "Upstarts," he whispered.

He ate half a bagel lavishly covered with lox and cream cheese, as good as Barney G.'s he thought. He went upstairs for a snooze with his precious material. Spread out on the bed he decided he would paint his whale skeleton with hardware store paint and save money. He became half tumescent thinking about Kara sitting nude at his desk and more so at the image of Laurette's vulva pressed against the gray upholstery of his car's front seat.

PART III

CHAPTER 11

Clive woke at dawn having lost his self-importance. He didn't know where it had gone but it wasn't in him anymore. His first thought was that the arts had gotten along without him for centuries and would continue to do so. In the night he had looked at the distorted moon through each small pane of beveled glass on the door out in the hall. He had also seen a bird his mother called a bullbat or nightjar flying across the moon in search of night-borne insects. One had flown so close to his face the evening before on the patio he could hear the *chuff* sound of its wings. His thoughts were impacted by the idea that nothing looked like anything else, which gave a painter something to do through any number of lifetimes. He had only drawn until the age of ten but then began with both watercolors, caseins, and a minimal supply of oils. Why not repeat himself? By a decrepit seventy maybe he would do a series of pure abstracts on the phases of the moon, which had been so dominating in his consciousness but which had been barely noticeable in New York City. He had every reason to believe that he had allowed language and thought to betray him, so it would be an immense relief to paint and abandon language and thought. He had been talking about art for twenty years and felt that though someone had to clarify matters he had done his share and it was time to shut his mouth on the matter.

After eleven days back home he had felt an often painful homesickness for Manhattan, unavoidable after living there for nearly forty years. Of course the old home was familiar but he was definitely insufficient in the arena of sentimentality. He doubted if there were enough intelligent people in this area to maintain the kind of mutual coherence that civilization is said to offer, while in New York there was nothing in the realm of the cultural that wasn't immediately at hand. He had noted that in the past twenty years there were more articles on what were called "wilderness issues," but nearly always written from the vantage point of a university. He imagined that few indeed managed to live a solitary life without totally losing their sense of peripheries. When he was eleven he and his father had driven far north into Ontario and it was spooky to camp and fish in an area so remote from others. The fishing was fantastically good but was so easy it nearly became dreary. They filled a big cooler with fillets and dumped the guts down a trail and watched a black bear and her cubs devour the feast. Another boon was the dawn mist on the lakes that reminded Clive of a Japanese art book in the Big Rapids library.

On a more ordinary level, and certainly an item to reduce self-importance, was the homesickness for real bagels, the stray hot dog with kraut on emerging from the museum in the late afternoon. In order to maintain equilibrium in New York City and to be taken seriously you had to maintain appearances whether you were teaching, giving a lecture, or evaluating a collection. In March he had looked through a grand sheaf of eighteenth-century French drawings for a Park Avenue widow and he could see that he had increased his credibility by wearing a soft, rumpled cashmere sport coat with a beige linen shirt, and a droopy Spanish bow tie he had bought in Cordoba. The widow was in her late sixties but had become uncomfortably girlish when they had a Ricard pastis at the end of the art chore.

Back home his dominant duty was to escort Mother to a bird-watching perch at daylight. He wore jeans and rubber boots and a heavy sweatshirt to protect against the clouds of mosquitoes. The dawn was loud with the admittedly pleasant chatter of birds. He then would sit on the patio and drink a pot of coffee waiting for her whistle which he wouldn't be able to hear in the house away from the mosquitoes. The odor of the insect repellent affected the taste of the coffee and the books by Sebald and Bolaño didn't quite fit in the current landscape and he fell back on rereading Bachelard's *The Poetics of Space,* a favorite from his college years.

Installing a lock on his bedroom door and painting the whale skeleton with a three-inch brush took the same amount of time. While putting a finishing touch on the spine straight above his head he tipped off the rickety ladder and there was a split second of panic before he landed harmlessly on the bed, which he had moved so that his head on the pillow at dawn would be facing out an open window, the better to see the world assume its particular shapes.

He napped a couple of hours awakening in the late afternoon delighted with the whale skeleton surrounding him. Now he was living in an enclosure worthy of his imagination. He heard lilting female voices and laughter and leaned to take a concealed peek out a side window at the patio. It was mother, Laurette, and Lydia drinking wine. Of course they knew each other as country neighbors but neither his sister Margaret nor his mother would mention Laurette out of respect for his absurd and ancient wounds.

When he clumped down the stairs to greet them all his heavy steps made him wonder how much self-importance you needed to get by. With too much heaviness he might break through the earth where the crust is thin.

He made himself a gravely needed martini and was slightly irritated looking up to a shelf where he spotted a blue cookie jar. The problem in his childhood was that when you stuck your hand in the jar you couldn't get it out with more than one cookie. Life was like that but then he chose not to dwell on a possible metaphor. Just stick to the cookies, bub.

Out on the patio the three women were watching two female cedar waxwings tugging at opposite ends of a piece of yarn. It was nesting material, his mother said, and she had been observing the quarrel for a solid hour. Laurette was standing and twisting at the hips because her back was sore. Lydia was sitting in a low-slung chair showing a lot of thigh in her short summer skirt. Even more prepossessing was a casserole of lasagna she had brought over which was on a table beside an empty wine bottle. The smell of the garlic and tomato sauce, Lydia's thighs, and the sunlight dappling through the willow tree overwhelmed him and he drank deeply.

"You look like a slob. You got paint on your face," Laurette said. She led him into the back of the garage. "I saw it here when I helped your sister paint her bedroom."

He quickly finished his martini in fear that she would dribble some paint remover into the drink. Now she was very close to him as she daubed at his face. Over her shoulder he could see the waxwings still tugging at the yarn, a metaphor of female tenacity but mostly a simple bird tug-of-war. He found himself pressing her against the hood of his mother's car, trying to kiss her but she averted her face. His hands kneaded her buttocks and he was becoming hard at an amazing speed.

"Jesus Christ, I have to think about this. I can't fuck you in a garage with people outside." She slipped away laughing.

"Why?" he said glumly. He stood there waiting for his penis to slump. It seemed comic at best that this woman could still bowl him over after forty years. How wonderful it would be to find a '47 Plymouth and paint her slouched in the corner with her pleated skirt up.

CHAPTER 12

The next morning while escorting his mother back from one of her birding sites he admitted to himself that he felt good. He knew his brain seemed to be melting but then he at least had some solid plans. It was a delight to wake in the near dawn dark and see the whale skeleton take shape and then there was the intended upcoming painting of Laurette in the car seat, and the portrait from memory of Kara of Fort Wayne, plus the 110 small paintings of the world through the small panes of beveled glass. And at first light he had had the additional perception about shape. He had stared through the window at a close-by willow slowly achieving its shape and speculated that humans were more like willows than other mammals, even the vaunted chimpanzee with whom our genome was 98 percent similar. Willows had that basic trunk body but then they were up for grabs with dozens of protruding limbs and heavy foliage. They simply sprawled in their lives like humans.

At breakfast, oatmeal and a not ripe banana, which made him crave his New York greengrocer, he became distressed because though she denied it his mother wasn't feeling up to snuff. It was her atrial fibrillation, unsteady heartbeat, which made her weaker and pale. When he managed to get her to try a bagel with cream cheese and lox she perked up a bit but then admitted that he should run her into the cardiologist after she lay down for a while.

He was disappointed because he wanted to get at his beveled glass painting now that his Masonite rectangles were dry, and then he was embarrassed by his disappointment. After all, he was here to take care of his mother not save what was left of his life, the rock bottom of his intentions. With the situation The Great Doubt began to arise, something that had been with him most poignantly for six decades or so, both philosophically and politically: the conviction that mayhem rules and nothing solidly constructive can be done about anything. This was mostly a mental infirmity borne up under by intellectuals, artists, and writers, but then Clive qualified somewhere in the middle.

Rather than starting then stopping painting he decided to clean out the culvert under the driveway near the gravel road. His mother had taken to leaving daily notes on this duty which did turn out to lessen The Great Doubt lump in the throat. The water-packed detritus was nearly all weeds, leaves, sticks, and gravel which he was able to pull out with a potato fork. At the beginning a large rabbit burst out of the culvert and in his surprise he yelled and threw himself sideways then felt silly but amused. His mother heard his yell and came out to check and laughed to hear of his rabbit attack.

The trip to the doctor's was pleasant. Near the office there was a McDonald's and he decided to have the first one of his life, an act of courage for a gourmand. The burger couldn't help but be unsatisfactory but the french fries were passable. As luck would have it he saw the same girl with the lovely rump coming down the street and felt a tickle in his nuts. At sixty the sexual urge comes and goes but is definitely there when called on. There was that old Freudian dictum that art is caused by repressed sexuality, and if so, he was definitely ready to paint. While waiting his mind segued to his mother's mother who was handsome but born deaf. He speculated about the silence his mother grew up within. She must have grown up talking to the radio which she still did to the NPR station. She came out of the doctor's office smiling and announced that she might very well live several more years.

Back home he was thrown off by a large FedEx package from Sabrina. He was hoping for some San Francisco food delicacies but the contents were a contemporary artist's coffee table book in two volumes, and a single massive book on Caravaggio, both published by Taschen. To Clive, Caravaggio was the single most intimidating artist in history so he put the books on top of the upright piano in the living room, out of range of his immediate notice. Sabrina's note said: "I remember hearing you talk about this guy when I was little." Indeed.

He stood near the door to the upstairs feeling as he often did that his consciousness was rushing past him at a rate that exceeded that of a suitable life. The grand thing about painting was that your mind slowed to the pace of the work at hand or you simplyy couldn't paint well. He decided to take a half hour walk like he used to do in the city when he was overexcited and would walk from SoHo up to Washington

Square and back.

He chose the open pasture across the road, drifting this way and that, a little concerned that his thoughts would begin with his daughter, then to his mother, to Margaret in Europe, but then to Susann, a painter friend of his in college who had died from a brain tumor a few years before. Way back when he was the star of his college art department, largely thought to be the most gifted student, tempestuous, full of Sturm und Drang, full of pronouncements, and with a coterie of three girls and a gay student, Robert, following him around and hanging on whatever he wished to say. Clive, however, and an observant art history professor knew a secret: Susann was a better painter. She was shy and deferential and lived out her life in obscurity up near Glen Arbor in Leelanau County. She painted sublimely, mostly landscapes, watercolors, and he had tried without success to get her a New York gallery. They were only in touch every year or so, and on a few of her infrequent trips to New York. She would always say, "Don't worry about me, I'm fine." She, in fact, did sell well in her locale but to Clive, Susann represented the grotesque unfairness of the art world, how someone as good as Susann could be totally ignored.

He owned three of her paintings and a few watercolors and when she died he had to put her work in a closet for a year to avoid his anger.

He walked the circumference of the twenty-acre pasture fence line across the road. There were about a dozen Angus mothers and their calves in the pasture and one of the calves chose to follow along behind him like a dog. He enjoyed the company.

"I am not your leader," he turned and said to the calf, which reminded him of another friend, a childhood calf who with his father's permission he took along on walks in the ten-acre woodlot on the southwest corner of the farm, part of a forty his mother had sold early on to pay for her college degree.

Now he was speculating whether or not Laurette would pose half-nude on the car seat. The whole idea was preposterously silly but why not? It was no more cheeky than the idea of his resuming painting. Part of the grace of losing self-importance was the simple question "Who cares?" More importantly, he didn't want to be a painter, he only wanted to paint, two utterly different impulses. He had known many writers and painters who apparently disliked writing and painting but just wanted to be writers and painters. They were what Buckminster Fuller might have called "low-energy constructs." Clive didn't want to be anything any longer that called for a title. He knew how to paint so why not paint. Everybody had to do something while awake.

When he got back to his whale room he e-mailed Laurette asking if she would pose then hastily did a seven-by-nine of a particularly dense clump of pale green willow branches, more than vaguely abstract as you would have to be a willow fan to have any idea what you were seeing. Before bedtime he did the same clump of willow branches through a pane of beveled glass with the moon behind it that was even more inscrutable. As he dropped off to sleep he was as delighted with the smell of his oil paints as a dog would have been with a freshly butchered shin bone.

CHAPTER 13

In the morning after his bird-watching duties he checked his laptop and Laurette had answered with her consent to posing but adding that the entire painting must be done in her presence so that he couldn't "Skype" it and put it on the Internet in which case she might lose her job. Of course this startled him what with his possible motives being "impugned" as people say. He made himself busy concocting a fib to his mother saying how nice it would be if they could drive around in the countryside in an old Plymouth like the one Dad had bought in the late fifties. A '47 Plymouth seemed unlikely in 2010, but then the idea of compromise was scarcely estranged from art. His mother was happy at the idea and said that finding an old car was no problem in a county full of her farmer acquaintances who hated to dispose of anything, thus the term "car gardens" for the barnyards full of disused cars and farm equipment.

The plot was clearly hatched and Laurette came up earlier on Friday than usual. In the three-day interim he painted seven of the beveled glass images, none of them quite satisfying which didn't disturb him. On impulse he also painted a portrait of the bullbat crossing the moon which he gave to Mother. Since a bird was involved she was touched. She said during the fall migrations she would sit outside on still nights and listen to the birds fly south, and on especially moonlit nights she did so for hours.

The ride in Frank McWhirter's '58 Chrysler was a bit much for Clive to handle. First of all they had gone early in the morning right after his mother's bird-watching. The weather was quite chilly and she insisted that he keep the front windows open so she could hear the birds. She was well bundled up and he wasn't. The fan on the car heater couldn't be on high which would interfere with her hearing so consequently he was warm from the waist down while shivering above with a cold chest and ears. It was not lost on him that this morning ride was a hoax organized to paint half-nude Laurette, a karmic payback as his ex-wife called it.

They drove slowly on gravel roads with his mother as delighted as he was morose.

His bad move among others was eating too much of the Sloppy Joe mixture the evening before, which was made of burger, undiluted tomato soup, cheddar cheese, and a dash of Worcestershire sauce. When she went in the toilet just before supper he had mischievously added another dash of Worcestershire, and she caught his indiscretion by sniffing the air.

"How could you, son? You know I can't handle spicy food."

"I'm sorry. In New York I eat spicy food and I miss it."

"I can't accept your apology. We'll have to cook separate meals."

This was good news indeed. She ate a full portion anyway with a tinge of the martyr. He added to his rebellion by using Tabasco he had found in his luggage, but then after going to bed at ten awoke at midnight sweating with indigestion. He tiptoed downstairs to pee and found his Gas-X in his Dopp kit. He foresaw insomnia and took the heavy Caravaggio back upstairs with him.

It had been ten years or so since he'd had a look at Caravaggio other than en passant at European museums. Now sitting cross-legged on his bed under the weak overhead light hanging between enormous rib bones he was immediately incredulous. He studied the boy embracing the goat for several minutes and then a horrifying detail of Medusa with its palpable black and gray snakes. His breath was short and there were goose bumps sweeping up his arms and shoulders and back and tears began to arise. What was happening to him, for Christ's sake? He was certainly staring at Caravaggio as a painter and not as a professor. He hadn't felt tears since a summer afternoon in New York so many years ago, when he had received a registered letter of his final notice of divorce. He had been ignoring Mozart's *Jupiter* on the radio but his sudden raw and vulnerable emotions allowed the music to truly enter his being so that he delaminated, the layers of him falling from each other.

It took an hour for him to calm down and lift the book from his sweating lap. It made a peeling sound and he wondered what a bright young writer struggling with his first work would feel on first reading *Hamlet* or Dostoyevsky's *The Possessed.* An explosion that would blow him through the window of his garret. He speculated on what might have happened if Caravaggio had been completely liberated from his Catholic subject matter and had been allowed to paint life herself, which he somehow managed to do without the high net of theological stricture. It occurred to him that only purity of intent would save his own sorry soul. If he were to continue to paint he had to do so without the trace of the slumming intellectual toting around his heavy knapsack of ironies. He was well into his own third act and further delay would be infamous.

CHAPTER 14

The crotch painting experience with Laurette was ponderously comic, though it took a while for Clive to gradually accept it as such. The first farcical conclusion was that you shouldn't try to paint with a hard-on. Painting was relatively nonmental but not *that* nonmental. What could he have been thinking? Nothing. Of course he was scarcely the first artist to try to make love to a model, but probably not a model who had been the first and most overwhelming love of his life. The fact that this love was only minimally requited made it even more painful and devoutly irrational. He flipped over in his mind dozens of novels he had read with their uniformly miserable stories of first love, the most harrowing being Knut Hamsun's *Victoria,* the ultimate in high-grade tearjerkers.

Laurette beeped her yellow Jeep when she passed and Clive drove over midway on a cloudy afternoon with his sketchbook, easel, and oils in the antique blue Chrysler. He had told Laurette he wouldn't be finished until late Saturday but she had insisted that the painting would never leave her house. He was mulling over the idea of a Duchamp effect where he would possibly paint her front and bare bottom layered on the same patch of two-by-three-foot canvas.

She was giddy as a girl when he arrived, puffing on a joint and sipping at a largish glass of nasty Californian chardonnay. He would have to wait for his own alcohol until the sketch was just so. The props were correct: green skirt, sandals, white sleeveless blouse with a circle pin. She was pissed when he asked her to remove her makeup and dampen her hair because she had been night swimming forty-two years before. Ideally he would have worked after dark but the dome light of the Chrysler was burned out and the idea of finding a replacement was unlikely.

Laurette disappeared to redo her face and hair and Lydia looked at him coldly from the sofa, her legs akimbo as usual.

"You shouldn't try to screw her. She had a hysterectomy this winter. I mean even if she wants to it wouldn't be a good idea."

"Oh really?" Clive said. He was unsure

what a hysterectomy was. He suddenly felt fragile and his skin tingled with absurdity. There was a sense of jet lag here with all emotions being unstablized. Where was the poetry in the experience? On dozens of trips to Europe after landing at dawn and the cattle drive at customs he'd walk a great deal to readjust his inner clock. If he was in Modena it was simply sitting for a coffee at a café in the village square and then buying some fruit for his room at the grand market. In London it was walking on the Thames along Cheyne Walk, and in Paris at the Luxembourg Gardens where he would recheck the topiary fruit trees. At the moment he was high and dry with his motives of redeeming his preposterous early love for Laurette. He had the idle thought that he could construct a university course to be called "Retarded Romanticism."

He had drawn up the Chrysler near the broken barn door and the sketching went well. The clouds were dark enough to be helpful and he had to turn on the car and heater to keep half-nude Laurette warm. He reflected again how some women maintain their bodies so well while men become beefy sluggards. When she had pulled up her skirt and removed her panties he stopped breathing and then hyperventilated.

He got out of the car and wandered around for a few minutes to calm himself. What was sillier he thought than a sixty-year-old man standing in a barnyard with a hard-on? He would have preferred that Laurette remain silent but allowed her to chatter, which was giving him a headache.

"When Keith and I decided to call it quits I went to Grand Valley and took a business degree. I guess you could say I got over-active with college boys and instructors and suchlike and then one day I said, 'Slow down girl.' Why am I screwing younger men with me in my thirties? Then I had this affair with a high school football coach who kept telling me he was going to leave his wife for me when she got well. But then he never did. It's an old story. Then I see a photo of her in the *Grand Rapids Press* for winning a 10K race. That's sick? I was so hurt I tried to stay away from all men. I mean I didn't stop on the proverbial dime as they say. I even had a short run with a black piano player then I read that a lot of musicians get AIDS which naturally scared me. So I finally went on the sexual wagon for a few years. I worked hard and went up the ladder in the company. I was a tough girl. I needed affection so I had a few affairs with other career women. Does this shock you?"

"No. A lot of people try everything." He was struggling with her knees and the way she crooked the toes in her sandals inward. He was relieved that he was now only semi-tumescent, which she also seemed to notice.

"I suppose so. I mean finally the whole sex thing wore me out mentally. Once you get in the company you travel a lot and work long hours. I mean Lydia is mostly just a friend and companion. She's bisexual but she has liberated herself from everything to help her poetry. Do you still want me? It sure seemed like you did in the garage. I mean I have some problems but we could fool around."

"Of course I do. I couldn't tell you why. I feel like a seventh grader and we're going to practice kissing." His hands were trembling and he pushed his sketchbook aside. She crouched over him on the big seat and they kissed. She took out his penis and rubbed it briskly against herself. He was off in a very short minute and he felt his heart and mind slump within himself.

"You must have saved up too long." She laughed.

He stared straight ahead as she patted herself with Kleenex, and then she grabbed the sketchbook and whistled. "You're the real thing," she said kissing his cheek.

CHAPTER 15

At a restorative dinner with Mother of meat loaf, baked potatoes, and stewed tomatoes he announced that he was painting a "sort of portrait" of Laurette.

"I can't wait to see it," she said.

"That's unlikely. I mean it's a very private painting. She was half-nude."

"I'd bet a dollar it wasn't her idea. Isn't it time you got over the sex thing? But I'm glad you're painting again. Way back when you were an artist you were happier. You'd come out for a summer visit with Tessa and Sabrina and we'd have picnics and we drove up to Mackinac Island and stayed in a fancy hotel. Remember? When you became a big shot professor you always acted like you were at a funeral."

He couldn't answer. He was lost in the thought of when he first met Laurette. She was ten and had just moved in down the road. They were riding their bicycles toward each other on the gravel road. Clive had seen the moving van and was curious. Laurette had veered her bike toward his with a smile and he had gone over in the ditch scraping his arm. She hadn't stopped. He kept his wound hidden from his mother because he didn't want it doused with stinging methylate but his dad saw it when they were fishing. Clive explained and his dad had simply said, "The female can be a problem." Now staring down at his dinner with a rather bleak smile, but a smile nevertheless, he thought how his infatuation with Laurette had truly begun in her early teens when he was becoming a biological furnace. The mystery of it all was permanent in human behavior. A lesbian couple who were close friends had met at camp at fourteen and were still together fifty years later. What they call "puppy love" was still love and when the other didn't feel it the punishment was severe.

In the morning he waited until nine to be polite and then went over to Laurette's eager for work. They were still in bed but Lydia let him in grumpily and he set up his easel near a large south window for the light he needed. He began painting and let the world of his life disappear wherever. Lydia had been in a scanty nightie when she let

131

him in and he appreciated that she was wearing a robe when she brought a muffin. When he was younger he actually enjoyed Sabrina riding her tricycle naked around his big SoHo studio but Lydia was another matter.

He finished as best he could by five in the afternoon. He had only eaten half a sandwich, and when Lydia made him a drink he was wary of his empty stomach but she also brought some fine cheese, olives, and bread, pronouncing the work as "truly sexy." Laurette was nonplussed and blushing while she studied it at different angles as if looking for hidden meaning. Then she tearfully said the painting was "fine." He said that he would touch it up the next morning. He found his work unbearably close to home. At that moment his angry mother called saying that Margaret called from Florence wondering why they hadn't responded to the e-mails she sent from her laptop every morning for more than two weeks.

He rushed home and showed his mother twenty pages of Margaret's cranky rundown of her trip that was overall wonderful. She had now decided to spend a month a year in Europe splitting her time among France, Italy, and Barcelona. Mother was pleased to see occasional references to indigestion.

"That doesn't happen in my house," she would repeat. Despite her anger over not getting Margaret's e-mails due to his *neglect* Mother vowed the whole computer age was satanic. "What's wrong with writing letters?" she would ask plaintively.

At dinner Clive took his share of her spaghetti sauce and added garlic, onions, and hot chiles. Mother once again said that he was "ruining his stomach and taste buds," then she heard an oriole through the open window which immediately changed her point of view on life. She cocked an ear toward the open kitchen window, her face slackened and became introspective. He was, frankly, envious. Until she passed eighty she and a couple bird-watching friends would take several trips a summer camping out in remote places. He and Margaret had been naturally concerned about the old ladies camping but when he questioned her on the phone she had said, "Don't be stupid, son. You have to be on-site when they wake up at daylight." It occurred to him during his generic spaghetti that the only similar thing he had was the act of painting.

The next morning he waited until ten to go over to Laurette's to touch up the painting. It was still too early. They were terribly hungover and Lydia said that they got drunk and "made out" while staring at the painting. Laurette blushed and hissed, "Sshhhh." They were pleasant but subdued, with Laurette packing up because it was Sunday. He finished the touching up in an hour, reflecting that if he continued to want to paint a portrait of Kara, his old girlfriend from Fort Wayne, it would be far better to travel there and paint her from life. A private detective who catered to the art business once told him, "Everyone can be found if you know how."

On the way home he pulled off on the farm lane that was the inception of the painting so long ago. He was thinking about his apartment in the city and how a woman, a wealthy collector and museum addict from Atlanta, had offered him an extravagant price to sublet his apartment if he ever traveled for an extended period. He had cooked her lunch or dinner several times with her picking up the goodies from Balducci's or Dean & DeLuca. It wouldn't hurt to sublet half a year and go to a place where he could paint comfortably and live cheap. When he felt courageous in the near future he'd also call his accountant and see what he would receive if he retired early on his TIAA-CREF, the professors' retirement

fund. It would be heartbreaking to give up
his apartment, his true home, and he refused
to imagine life without it. If he got desperate he could get money from Sabrina but
the idea knotted up his pride.

CHAPTER 16

Clive wound down tightly into his painting
not himself. Mother was checking off the
kitchen calendar and announced every
breakfast the number of days before Margaret came home. Now it was nine. He had
no particular interest in the so-called natural
world but checked out willows on the Web,
noting that the Ainu, the primitive people
of Japan, considered willows to be of religious and magical significance. This meant
nothing to Clive who felt he had not a shred
of religion or superstition in his being. The
writers he knew could be goofy on this score
but rarely the painters who tended toward
the matter-of-fact. He could, however,
understand how the Ainu might be taken
by willows plus the Web said that willow
shoots could be made into an herbal tea for
killing pain. Deer devoured them after a
long winter partly to relieve themselves of
arthritic discomfort.

He made a number of visits a few miles down the road to a ten-acre woodlot where he used to hunt rabbits with his dad. It was pleasant to sit on a stump in a glade with his sketch pad and find something that caught his interest, often the osier, what most called dogwood, with the sweet smell of its tiny blooms, also the chokecherry tree with its overwhelming odor. He ended up kneeling and doing a series of close-up sketches of the white pine stumps on which he usually sat with their burn marks of a century-old fire that had hit the area. When he made the small painting it occurred to him that only students of stumps could have any idea what it was. On a rare warmhearted whim he did a small portrait of a bluebird for his mother then was embarrassed when she was overwhelmed.

"I'll cherish it forever, which probably won't be long," she said intensely.

Mother had been in a dither after talking on the phone several times. Sabrina would come for a few days of birding, then she would take her father camping in the Upper Peninsula when Margaret returned. Sabrina wanted to see the area where Louis Agassiz, one of her naturalist heroes, had traveled in the 1850s from Cambridge, Massachusetts. Like most people in Michigan Clive had never been to the U.P., then recalled there was that quick pass-through from St. Ignace to Sault Ste. Marie with his father on their Canadian fishing trip. The very idea put him on a short end. The last thing he wanted to do on earth was to camp. Maybe it would rain and they could stay in a motel. Why make yourself uncomfortable for no good reason? He calmed down when it occurred to him that Sabrina had organized the trip as a "rapprochement." One cause of his mother's excitement was that all of her bird-watching companions were dead and she considered her granddaughter her best friend on earth. Unfortunately, Sabrina's upcoming visit put his mother in a mental dither and she began talking about Dostoyevsky. She had taken a course in Russian literature and Margaret and Clive had learned to dread her Dostoyevsky monologues. Mother had written her term paper on *The Brothers Karamazov,* a book that some never recover from any more than certain painters don't get over Caravaggio. Her disquisitions on the Karamazov family always ended up with her own husband, "When the love of my life died . . ." and then she would break down. If she had concentrated on Turgenev it would have been easier on all of them. Once she had even called Clive Kolya, her favorite character in the book, after an ample glass of wine.

Clive's workday went from 6 a.m. to dinner at 6 p.m. He enjoyed the mental and physical exhaustion that owned none of the enervation of what he thought of as his real life. One day while sketching in the woodlot he was spooked by a female voice calling out his name several times. He had been sketching a small square of leaf litter with the tiny buds on fiddlehead ferns and was so deep within it that he had trouble emerging from it, but finally yelled "What?" with irritation. It was Lydia coming through a grove of young maples, wearing blue shorts and slapping at mosquitoes on her legs.

"I saw your parked car. I thought I'd stop to say hello." Now she was a little nervous at the slowness of response on his part.

"I was just sketching," he finally said, realizing that she was so far out of context in the woodlot that he was puzzled.

"You could stop by when you like." She was vaguely embarrassed which was so unlike her. "Laurette said I should offer you a little affection when you need it." She turned and walked quickly back toward the road.

"Thank you," he called out.

Now he had a bad case of the jitters and

sat down on a stump. Where was he anyway? Actually and literally buried in his work and without any sense of sexuality. In fancy terms he had abandoned his calling and now was resuming it. Soon he would be getting older, a daffy concept. He was a man of no importance so why not paint? He struggled to locate himself. There was Mother, Margaret, and Sabrina, with whom the upcoming reunion was the most important thing in his life along with simply painting. He thought momentarily of Tessa. Why had they beaten themselves up so badly after those years of towering ambition, a tree so tall it had to tip over? It was clearly his fault, the doom of ambition and marriage. Should he try to see her? Probably not. He should just paint and then the doors of the world are surprisingly open if you don't lock them.

Late in the afternoon he drove Mother over to a tavern on Chippewa Lake where she was going to meet an old friend to have hamburgers for supper. "I have one a year," she announced. When they got there he was relieved that she didn't mention that this was his father's favorite tavern.

The friend was a very old stooped man with a vigorous handshake named Orville.

"I was sweet on your mother. Good thing

she didn't choose me or you wouldn't exist." Orville laughed.

"Of course," Clive said. He was amused by the fragility of the idea.

While they chattered about the old days Clive's mind drifted to the lake out the front window. The season wasn't open yet, or so he thought, while envisioning a plate of bluegills and perch fried in butter. He and his father used to catch them on live crickets. There was no reason not to return in August and catch some fish, maybe paint one.

CHAPTER 17

Margaret arrived two days early because her traveling friend had had an illness in the family. She drove up from Grand Rapids with Sabrina, who had flown in from San Francisco the night before and had rented a ghastly-looking vehicle called a Hummer. When they came in the driveway before noon Clive was just emerging from the thicket where he had burned the remains of an old chicken coop on the west side and had vainly tried to make a series of sketches of the fire. Margaret joked that when Clive came out of the thicket she was frightened because he looked like Dad. In the next two days before Clive and Sabrina left for the north Margaret would let slip little phrases in Italian and French like people do who have just returned from Europe.

Sabrina startled Clive and he looked at her thinking she must be wearing high-heeled boots. She said she was six foot and when they embraced she was slender but athletic. Hadn't he been paying attention or had the world grown smaller in the three years since he had seen her? Possibly.

There were two days of family nonsense with Mother insisting that they play card games, canasta and hearts, since there were four of them. Clive was pleased that he didn't have to pack up all of his belongings because they were coming back to the farm. With this two-day interruption he was trying to keep art at a distance but was unsuccessful. Sabrina brought the past back freshly and he was slightly frightened at what had been happening to him in the few weeks on the farm. Was he ready to give up everything, but then it occurred to him he was giving up nothing that he cared about. He had called the rich woman in Atlanta. She was thrilled at the idea of subletting his apartment for half the year and the generous price she offered that took care of the whole year's rent. He called the accountant in New York and it was determined his retirement would be forty-six thousand a year, not much but not bad. Associates in Portland, Oregon, and Athens, Ohio, had offered short but well-paid teaching stints, and there was a full-time offer at Stanford but he couldn't bear to think of anything full-time. He would be a wandering painter half the year. In a college course on medieval Europe he had liked the idea of being a troubadour.

They played cards and drank wine late the last evening and he entertained them with comic stories of the lecture circuit and European travels. Once in a Paris hotel he had called the desk with his imperfect French and requested a foam pillow because feathered pillows made him sneeze. They brought him up an omelet. Once in St. Louis after giving his patented lecture on Art and Economics and during the Q & A, a persistent but well-dressed oaf who had his MBA written all over him tried to corner Clive into putting a price tag on the *Mona Lisa.* Clive refused by saying that the painting (which he didn't like) could be considered either worthless or priceless. It simply didn't matter since it would never be sold and price assumes a transaction. The young man who had obviously had a few drinks before the lecture had kept yelling "You're copping out" until he was asked to leave. At the door he had turned and bellowed "fuck you" and the audience had laughed.

"I hate that word," Mother said, cocking an ear toward the patio door and listening to a whip-poor-will, but Sabrina and Margaret laughed.

Mother had monopolized Sabrina's time with local bird-watching expeditions and stayed up for longer in the evening than was her habit so that Clive had had almost no opportunity to talk to Sabrina alone. Early on the morning that they left for the north he was standing in the driveway with her and they were circling around their three-year absence from one another but then the dog whistle blew back in the thicket. Sabrina grinned and took off at what Clive thought was an alarming speed to retrieve her grandmother.

In the silly Hummer heading north with Sabrina at the wheel Clive joked that the odor of the tuna fish sandwiches Mother had packed for them was "haunting."

"You seem happier than I ever remember," Sabrina said.

"I do?" Clive was startled by this. He imagined that he was tormented though in truth nearly all of his thoughts were directed to whatever he was painting rather than to his life problems.

"Grandma said that all you did was paint, though when I was a little girl painting never seemed to make you happy. You were always worried about your gallery."

He couldn't think of what to say about

the horrors of galleries so he changed the subject to her mother and after a short time Sabrina became tearful about her mother's *mood* pills. He had had his own experiences with Prozac but had given it up when his long city walks seemed to work without any additional help. Sabrina also talked about the responsibility of unearned income and he figured that it was the most singular reason she was working toward a PhD in earth sciences. Partly out of her reaction to her mother she simply enough wanted to lead a useful life.

The mordant conversation was broken at the Straits of Mackinac and the immensely high bridge gave Clive an attack of acrophobia. She laughed when he slumped low in his seat like a little boy. On the other side of the bridge they pulled into a rest stop and shared the tuna fish sandwiches with a cloud of seagulls. During lunch a strong wind rose from the northwest and Sabrina said she had checked and the weather looked very bad for camping the next two days but fine on the third and last day of their trip. She pulled over and fiddled with her BlackBerry making hotel reservations in Marquette and Clive felt rosy with relief after being spared from spending two nights in his mother's cheap sleeping bag and tiny tent.

They parked a few minutes in Munising and laughed at the sight of snow and sleet blowing in strongly off Lake Superior. Snow in late May seemed unreasonable but there it was. Sabrina had been giving him an intriguing lecture on the structure of the cosmos, which was largely beyond him with his diffident glance every Tuesday at the science section of the *New York Times*.

"The miracle is that the world exists," he intoned.

"My God, who said that?"

"Wittgenstein. I don't think it's an exact quote."

"How wonderful. Was he religious?"

"Not in the least," Clive said. "He also said 'I am my world.' "

"That's not so good," she said with a twisted frown.

It was almost eerie to see her at close range after three years' absence. How could he have been that buried in himself in what he now saw as his declining life? He couldn't very well say that he was on his way back up because that would be presumptuous but he definitely had changed directions. How could it have started with yellow paint on his prized possession, his English tailored suit? It was daffy as life itself. On the last trips to Mother's farm before the divorce, he and Sabrina would take long early morning walks on the property. She was maybe six at the time and wanted to hear stories about his boyhood. She would catch snakes, toads, frogs and examine them while he talked. Her curiosity about the natural world was insatiable.

When they reached Marquette late in the afternoon the city was loud with the roar of the storm on Lake Superior. The hotel, the Landmark Inn, was fairly sophisticated even by New York standards. He'd rather expected fishermen and loggers running amok. Sabrina had secured the Teddy Roosevelt suite plus an extra room in case someone needed to be alone. He was reminded again that his daughter was wealthy but it quickly occurred to him she didn't act like it. All of her clothing seemed aimed at her outdoor life and obsessions and her conversation when not geared to her mother was about the sciences.

He was staring at a series of photos of Teddy Roosevelt with a room service vodka in hand. He recalled reading a biography of Roosevelt and his fantastic hardiness in college, and how Roosevelt took his own Airedale dogs to Africa on a safari.

"Grandma said that you painted all day every day and you seemed quite happy doing so. You didn't really respond before," Sabrina said a little timidly behind him. "She said that it was quite a shock."

"I'm thinking of retiring and becoming a Sunday painter every day." He smiled blankly as if knowing it sounded a tad daffy.

When she headed off in foul weather gear for a beach walk he arranged his watercolors and sketchbook on a table near the window faced toward the northeast from which he could see the harbor ten stories below down a steep hill, and a break wall and tormented Lake Superior which reminded him of the painting of Winslow Homer. He stared down long and hard at the harbor, picked up his sketchbook, and then saw his daughter striding along far below and thought briefly of the distances at which we keep each other.

Two days later when the weather changed with the wind coming from the south he awoke in the tent thinking he had survived a night in the wilds. Sabrina sat by the campfire reading the Agassiz book, said good morning, and started making him breakfast. What would become of him? But then the task of thinking about himself was tiring like trying to comprehend the chaos theory in Science Times. Behind Sabrina there was a shade of green on a moss-colored log he had never seen before. And on that first afternoon in Marquette there had been a splotch of sunlight far out on the dark stormy lake, golden light and furling white wave crests. Time was passing as his daughter read and scrambled eggs. He had had his dream of the world's idea of success but it was surprisingly easy to give up for his first love.

■ ■ ■ ■

THE RIVER
SWIMMER

■ ■ ■ ■

PART I

Theirs was a small farm in the middle of an island in a large river started during the Great Depression when county and state land regulations loosened in the name of need. The Chippewa Indians vainly claimed it but then they perhaps justly claimed everything in the area. There was a lone old maiden Indian woman living there called Tooth because rather than having two prominent front teeth she had one very large one. She took care of the progenitor of the family and farm through the Depression when it was a survival property with a few cows and pigs fenced in by rushing water. The soil was magnificently fertile, alluvial, with a couple feet of topsoil. Simply everything grew and grew fast and irrigation water was easily diverted from the river during drought periods. Old Thaddeus married an English girl in the First World War but their second generation was a bit of a bust in terms of vigor. Thaddeus was an ex-logger and believed in twelve-hour work-days, six days a week, and on Sunday he fished the river. The second generation were a bit effete in his terms, three sons who were star high school athletes and a daughter named Marie Love who bore another Marie Love, both star workers with Grandpa. The girls, daughter and granddaughter, were the hard workers, the apples of his eye, so the three star athletes were left out of the will. The sole owner of the farm was the first Marie Love and then the second who was Thad's mother. He never knew the great-grandfather he was named for, a loud and mean and burly man with a false last name, Sockrider, from his youth of hauling sup-plies on mules to logging camps. Tooth, in fact, hung in there on the island because she was born there and felt she had a claim to the property. Her father had thought he owned it because he signed what he thought was a timber lease which was really a bill of sale, a common way that whites swindled Indians out of land, even beautiful lakes set in the middle of thousands of acres of forest and good farmlands. We could be uncom-fortably awful people. Tooth even showed old Thaddeus her family graveyard in a remote part of the island next to a vast virgin oak which he immediately intended to cut down and sell. He looked at the Anishinabe graves without comment and said he would take care of her in her old age. The reverse came true as she took care of him in his final bedridden years and the family too. Because of the rare honored treaty rights local Indians could shoot deer out of season and old Tooth was a good hunter shooting deer, grouse, ducks, and the occasional feral pig, necessary as they were destructive to the garden and crops.

Thad the boy grew up hyperactive and obnoxious as his father, an oil roustabout and oil fire fighter from Texas who appeared in the area during a big fire at the best well and seemed daring and romantic to young Marie Love to the disgust of her father who only cared for logs and crops. Marie and the southerner, Thetis by name, eloped and their son was improbably difficult as his mother was hardworking and his father was lazy in between trips to put out oil fires throughout the world. The Indian woman Tooth was the only one with any control of boy Thad. She created a play yard with an impenetrable electric fence to keep him out of the river. Such was his love of water he was always wet even in winter. Once when his father spanked him he stuffed his expensive cowboy boots with pig shit which stopped the spanking thing. In the summer of his third year when boy Thad taught himself to swim in the spring pond behind the farmhouse, Tooth devised a leather harness that allowed her to tether him to a stake while he swam and dove in the spring pool. If she thought he was holding his breath too long she could haul him screaming to the surface. His biggest special thrill was when his father fished the river in a rowboat with a small motor and let Thad swim at the end of a long rope to keep the current from sweeping him away. For a slender swimmer's body his chest grew very large as often happens. Luckily his school didn't have a swim team or he would have become a worthless star athlete though he drew the attention of the university when he swam to shore from the Manitou Islands and Beaver Island in Lake Michigan. To be frank he could not stop himself and that was his downfall.

Downstream a half dozen miles toward town the riverside property was taken up by the fancy small estates of men of good fortune in the area. One, an auto dealer, had hired Thad cheap to put in a vineyard for him. Rich men in the Midwest easily become obsessed with creating thoroughly mediocre if not awful wine. It's a bit like owning your own golf course. However our small town mogul quickly noted that his precious daughter Laurie was sweet on his vineyard boy and fired Thad. The auto dealer was known as Friendly Frank as he would occasionally sell a car or pickup at wholesale on impulse. Despite this he was improbably vigilant about his daughter. Friendly Frank was a closet case and knew the young man was beautiful and had coupling primarily in mind and Laurie didn't dress modestly. It was either very short summer skirts or bikinis down on the big dock in front of his barbecue shack which was a giant wine barrel standing upright with a door to a round room holding his smoker and a cot with a sleeping bag where he would spend the night drinking when he smoked meats that took a long time, maybe twelve hours. Now Frank peeked through an air vent and there was Laurie, a fifth-year ballet student in a bikini with the toes of her right foot kneading Thad's shoulder. Frank bellowed, "Laurie, stop that!" Laurie turned without taking her toes off Thad's shoulder.

"Dad, stop spying on me. It's creepy."

"Young man, I told you not to come back here. You're trespassing."

"Dad, he was swimming past. I waved him in. We're in geometry together."

"I told you this place is off limits for this swim farmer, and I discover you showing him your bare ass."

"You're disgusting," Thad said and Friendly Frank forced his way in the small door and grabbed a barrel stave from the kindling box of the smoker and swung it hard against Thad's cheekbone which shattered and blood poured from his mouth. Thad dropped to his knees groaning. "Dad, you killed him," she screamed. Frank kicked his daughter out of the away and dragged Thad out the door to throw him off the dock. Frank had played defensive end for Notre Dame, the home of many car dealers. Laurie grabbed her father around the knees and he stumbled. Thad nearly unconscious grabbed an ankle with both hands. Frank fell on his face hard on the dock planking but was able to kick Thad off the dock's edge where he began to float away with strobe lights flashing on his head. Laurie thought he was imperiled and jumped in the river after him with her father shouting, "No!" Laurie didn't swim well but Thad was conscious enough to tow her to shore and push her onto a sandbar. Frank made his way to the sandbar and lifted her up where she struggled against him wildly. Frank looked down at Thad as if puzzled. He lifted a huge foot as if to stomp down on Thad's neck but first pitched Laurie up in some bushes on the bank where she was safe. Thad waved and shouted "stay" and the foot came down. He grabbed the foot and twisted violently and Frank fell back into the current and drifted off facedown. Thad swam quickly past him with the bright lights continuing to burst on his head. He thought of drowning Frank and dove under him pulling him deep by his belt. Frank struggled and Thad had the sudden idea that this act would make him as bad as Frank. He let go of the belt and Frank floated to the surface and began drifting. He would let him drown by himself though with his bulk he would float well. Thad knew he was within a quarter of a mile from a big eddy and channel where he regularly camped and had some gear. Laurie had met him there two days before in her little motorboat. They had necked dangerously in their bathing suits then nude. She had laughed at his efforts to put on a condom then did it with her mouth. She said it was how whores did it or so she had read in one of her dad's dirty magazines. He had done it with a few other girls but none so explosive as Laurie. Now he kept his imperfect eyes open for the eddy leading to the channel to the lagoon and camping spot. For some reason he could see better than ever before under water, small solace for his blasted cheekbone which crunched when he spit out a volume of water and ached like hell herself.

A devout student of natural history, he received the shock of his life when he reached the lagoon. The lagoon had always offered a great concentration of frogs and polliwogs and now they were traveling in thick shimmering circles. Here and there a water baby would swim in, sip, and swallow a polliwog with a smile. They were about eight inches long with normal baby features and dark hair and pinkish skin. Thad shouted under the surface and choked on water. He was so frightened he threw himself up on the bank sobbing for breath. He had never been more confused and was shaking from head to toe. He was further shocked hearing a voice.

"Thad, I am dying."

He looked up and there was Frank standing chest high in the water in the channel to the lagoon. He was shivering violently and barely conscious. The last bit of twilight shimmered off his reddish hair and badly bruised face from falling on the dock. His obviously fractured nose was swollen almost comically it was so large.

"You look awful, Thad. I hit you hard. The cheekbone is like a muskmelon."

"Come over here and I'll start a fire in my campsite."

"I can't move but I've seen her shampoo at your campsite. You're a bastard. She's my little girl. I'll kill you if she's pregnant."

"Enough of killing. I could let you die where you are."

Thad quickly waded over, took his arm, and led him on a path through a thicket to a small campsite. He untied a rope and lowered his cache in a big black plastic bag. He quickly started his fire pit going with a chunk of white pine stump and fir kindling. He put down a dry cloth called a space blanket and the fire was soon roaring. He told Frank to get out of his wet clothes. He did so and looked at Thad with fury.

"I can smell her scent on the blanket."

The sleeping bag was as close as it was safe to the fire and Frank was half dozing and mumbling, "The sheriff's water rescue boat will come. We shouldn't say anything that would complicate matters."

"Maybe I should tell them that you peek at her all the time."

163

"She's adopted," Frank yelled.

"That changes nothing."

Upriver they could see spotlights flashing against the trees and bushes that bordered the river. Someone cut the jet boat engine and hollered, "I smell campfire."

"I'm going to run for it."

"Good idea. Do you have any money?" Frank offered him a wad of wet cash. "Stay away and there'll be more. Just call."

Thad put the money in a plastic water-proof bag he carried when swimming to town. He was hungry and wanted pork chops at the diner but knew he couldn't chew. He entered his impenetrable thicket. The jet boat had a shallow draft and entered the lagoon to see if Frank was alive. Thad thought it must horrify the water babies. His English grandmother read him the story which he didn't care for. The Indian Tooth told stories of infant water spirits who when they died on earth some entered birds but most lived in water to keep away from people who were dangerous.

Thad heard the sheriff's high-pitched voice, "Frank, who did this to you?"

"No one. I fell on the dock face-first then rolled off and started drifting downstream."

"Where's Thad? Your daughter said he had a camp down here."

"I knew it. This is our land. I was lucky to find it in the dark and get a fire started."

The rescue people rolled Frank onto a floating stretcher which they lifted into the jet boat. Thad sat close by in the middle of the thicket glad they hadn't brought a search dog. Their lights moved away; the big jet boat cranked up and moved away. Thad thought it would scare the water babies. He realized knowing the culture that their secret must be kept forever. He recalled the many stories Tooth had told him as a child and still did. She had lived her whole life as an Anishinabe (Chippewa-Ojibway) on the river. And one thing she claimed was that no infants actually die. They live in the water as fish, or in the woods as birds, sometimes hidden in the water in human form around the summer solstice. His skin prickled when he remembered the clear eyes of the babies. He recalled that he asked Tooth if big fish eat babies. She said, "No, they're relatives but water babies eat minnows, polliwogs, mayflies, caddis, and other insects." Tooth insisted that if they ever returned to full human form it was their choice. He wished he could talk to Tooth but now was the time to run for it. Too much could go wrong. Frank could change his story or Laurie could say something wrong. The whole event was confusingly violent.

He swam to shore and walked the road barefoot without a problem. The soles of his feet were hard and callused because as a swimmer he avoided shoes whenever possible. He could even run on the school's cinder track barefoot. There were too many lights and too much traffic when he came close to town so he slipped down the bank to the river only getting out when he came close to the dam. His broken cheekbone still hurt like crazy so he stopped at a Dairy Queen and drank two chocolate milk shakes. The cold hurt but was tolerable. On the other side of town he swam the remaining four miles to Lake Michigan. Because of the increased pitch of land the current increased. Luckily he had certain boulders memorized and he shortly reached the mouth of the river where there were several campfires of night fishermen. In exchange for telling them about his secret cache of firewood he was invited to share their fire. They were middle-aged men and as soon as they got a good look at him in the firelight they began talking fast. "Jesus Christ, where did you come from?" "Who clubbed you?" "Has there been a crime," and so on. "The police should be called."

"They were. But I wouldn't sign an assault complaint. I started it."

That calmed them down. A gray-haired man moved near Thad. "Unfortunately I'm an oncologist not an orthopedist. You should be sent to the E.R. I just recognized you. You're the kid last August that broke a record by swimming from Ludington to Milwaukee to raise money for charity. So why aren't you smart enough to go to the E.R.?"

"I'm on the run. I'm going to swim down to Chicago."

The men were boggled. The oncologist touched Thad's wound and he winced saying, "I can feel the fracture in the zygomatic bone. I have some doctor friends in Chicago. You can disappear there. They'll treat you free. Our friend swam for the University of Michigan. He won a bronze at the Olympics."

"I was never interested in competing." Thad felt shy.

"Why, it's the American way. We never stop competing."

"Well, I'd work all day on our farm on the island in the river. I'd dive in at lunch and at the end of the afternoon for an hour or so. It's the most complete feeling of freedom that there is. The current guides your skin.

It's the closest we get to a bird. I was always obsessed with birds and fish since childhood. I just want to feel at home on earth."

The men looked at Thad as if he were daft.

"We're in Muskegon. It's over a hundred miles to Chicago. I will give you a ride to town and spot you a ticket."

"I sort of want to enter by water. I can do it in a couple of days. I will sleep in Saugatuck and Gary, to spend the night with cousins and take some liquids. I still can't chew."

"But why?" asked the oncologist.

"Because it's what I love best. I generally prefer rivers but Lake Michigan works. I studied conditions today and as you noticed it's an offshore wind so the water is warmer. Hypothermia is your main enemy. You can't think logically. Your blood sugar is low among other things."

"I admire you. Do what you want. *Fais ce que tu voudras,* as the French say," said the least vocal of the fishermen, drinking from a pint of schnapps. "These guys make a lot of money but they haven't done shit. Keep the Lexus washed. I didn't do much but when I was fourteen I rode my bicycle to the Upper Peninsula, then way over west to Duluth with a friend camping all the way. These were balloon tire bikes."

"We've heard this before," a fellow fisherman said.

"Well, hear it again. What the fuck have
you done? Go to Princeton and trade stocks.
In a good society you would have been
executed three years ago."

"Another rich radical. Big deal."

"Sure I put six nephews and nieces
through college and I only got a few million
left to fish on. Remember when I cracked
up a few years ago? I fished ninety days in a
row. Not a dime for a shrink. I am like the
kid here. It's water that heals a man!"

It was near dawn before they turned in.
The men shared their extra bedding with
Thad and he awoke to a half dozen
scrambled eggs he could get past his jaw.

In a modest imitation of a Viking rite they
all walked down to the turbulent outflow of
the river. He plunged in and disappeared in
a trice into the current and wave chops. The
men stood there in a state of melancholia as
if they had lost an appealing space visitor
with his wrist wallet and a plastic pack of
clothing at the back of his waist.

"A great man," the oncologist intoned to
the embarrassment of the others.

Meanwhile Thad was at home again, heading south toward Chicago, a thrilling place
he had visited with his parents, especially

the aquarium, also a city mostly surrounded by the fact of water. He and his father had walked along Lake Michigan while his mother shopped. His father had inherited ten thousand dollars from a maiden aunt and wanted a new car while his mother wanted the money saved for Thad's education. He heard their night quarrels with disgust. His dad said, "He can swim his way through college." The local superintendent knew some of the coach staff at Michigan State, his own alma mater, and the swimming coach had visited. Thad's dad had driven him to a local lake and he had swum a measured hundred yards within a couple of seconds of the Big Ten record, and then holding back for reasons of orneriness. The coach said he had a *free ride* but Thad had his heart set on Scripps in California for the oceanography program if he went to college at all. If only there was a college with an oceanography program on the banks of a big beautiful river. His interests were pure and simply singular. He had thought of lowering his aim to hydrology but that seemed too mechanical. If there were indeed water spirits they had a firm hold on him like love eventually does on young men, an obsessional disease of sorts.

He drew close to Saugatuck by early

evening, went ashore for his chocolate milk shake, and called his cousin's cell. It was a warm early evening and the beaches still had the lovely girls sprawled this way and that drinking beer. He had been somewhat embarrassed by how attentive his father had been to the bathing beauties of Chicago but supposed it was male nature. His cousin Rick showed up in a tuxedo jacket and swim suit with three delicious girls and made an extravagant entrance. Family gossip said he dealt drugs and had gotten arrested. Rick said he had talked to his mother who had said that Thad's father had gone to town and kicked Frank's ass after hearing of the clubbing from his daughter who was friendly with Thad's mom. The fight took place in the parking lot of the mall near the auto dealership. The police didn't arrest Thad's father because Friendly Frank had tried to use a tire iron as a weapon and there was a sense of fair play. Thad was upset because he wanted this matter to be over despite his swollen face.

They went to Rick's obviously expensive condo. He said he was cooking a roast beef for Thad's swimming energies. The three girls were spread out in the bedrooms and Thad figured he was destined for the sofa unless he got lucky though he needed sleep more than sex. Rick had taken him aside and explained the females were rich girls from Winnetka near Chicago who were there basically for cocaine.

He took a very long hot shower to get warmth back in his body stolen by the water. His jaw wasn't feeling nearly as bad and he hoped to get something solid in his body.

The bathroom was dense with steam. He heard the door open and within moments the diminutive girl Emily slipped into the shower. She had told him that she was a poet and he didn't know what to say never having met anyone who introduced them- selves as a poet. She was a peculiar lisper and had just spent a first year at Sarah Lawrence. She admitted she was with a *fast crowd* of childhood friends. He wasn't partial to poetry until recently a young teacher in an American literature class had him read a book called *Desert Music* by Wil- liam Carlos Williams which he liked, a waterless book. He kissed the top of her head and looked down her back at her pretty bottom.

"I've never been this impulsive but I didn't want you to get away," she whispered. They coupled on the bathroom rug then sat there feeling shy.

"Rick said you are a farmer and a swimmer. I don't get the connection."

"Just that one body does both."

"Don't swim at downtown beaches when you get to Chicago. The water isn't clean. Come up to our place. The water is cleaner north of town."

"I'll have to swim up there. I don't have a car."

"I'll pick you up or send a cab. Where you going to live?"

"I've no idea. I'll get a room."

"I like the way you talk. You don't talk snotty like boys I know. Make sure you get a room in a nice neighborhood."

He deduced that she was a rich girl and he had only met a few and found them otherworldly.

"I've never felt in danger."

"You have knuckles but they have guns downtown."

At dinner the other two girls acted catty that Emily had snared this available male. She enjoyed feeding him lots of small bites of rare roast beef and French potato salad that his jaw allowed. The bathroom mirror had revealed an appallingly purple cheek which made him think he would call the oncologist's friend.

It was just at dawn, 4:30 a.m., and he was

hearing the first warbler when Emily covered him again. She certainly was eager but he was anxious to get started in order to get there before dark.

"I'm a little sore," she whispered.

"Not my fault," he joked.

"Asshole," she hissed.

In the kitchen he gathered his stuff and drank a quart of milk. Oddly you could get dehydrated while swimming. It was a warmish dawn with calm seas on Lake Michigan. Emily waded in in her nightie and kissed him good-bye. She had engraved her cell number on his forearm deeply with a ballpoint pen. Though it was late he was feeling a tinge of guilt about Laurie back home but then what do you do when a lovely girl steps into the shower with you. He and Laurie had been close for seven years, since the fourth grade. Her parents, the mighty Frank and frowsy Barbara, were snobs and favored the son of a privately wealthy physician, Isaac, who was headed for Yale in the fall. The doctor was Frank's partner in the pathetic wine business. Laurie's conversation tended to be dominated by stories of her father's bullying rages. Now in the water swimming south he waited for the rhythm of his strokes to disperse the embarrassing images of Laurie and Emily whirling together as if one couldn't tell them apart which wasn't fair to either he thought. So often Laurie was morose about her parents that it was hard to be with *normal* young people. To Thad, her father Frank was an all-out loudmouthed bully who had portrayed himself as having been a football hero at Notre Dame. How much was true no one seemed to know. He was very large and had played defensive end. It occurred to Thad that there were other examples in town and when he had asked his dad about it his dad had said Texas was full of "loudmouthed assholes" of that origin. He said that he and his oil roustabout friends liked to kick the asses of these college jerks in bars. In truth his family had come from a failed small ranch in the Panhandle and he and his brothers had moved to the oil fields. They were lanky and strong but purposefully soft-spoken. Early on he had taught Thad counterpunching and the loose chokehold to avoid bullying. A crisis had been Frank beating his wife on the butt with a board for ordering too many things from catalogs, which so humiliated her mother that she wouldn't leave her room for three weeks. This was nearly inconceivable to Thad and made Laurie weepy and maudlin, but when asked why her mother didn't leave him she couldn't speculate other than she loved her home, a virtual mansion that Thad thought looked silly.

He had underestimated his time and distance and still had quite a ways to go at twilight when the lights of Chicago sparkled to the south. He swam to shore and was lucky enough to find a smoldering beach fire that he stoked and a damp blanket he held up to dry out a bit. He recalled that recently while watching boxing with his father he had said authoritatively that champions never screw the day before a fight and he didn't care to tote up how many times he and Emily had gone at it. He gummed at some soft cheese and bread from his pack despite the strong twinge in his jaw. He didn't dare chance a pain pill because of its normally soporific effects. He slept hard and was back in the water before daylight. South of Gary he swam over the top of a huge ore freighter wash which was similar to an ocean comber. He was close enough to see clearly men on the freighter's deck. He waved but they didn't notice him. He was also alert to swim counter to the growing boat traffic and their fatal props. By noon he could see the Sears Tower clearly and was amazed at the plane traffic using O'Hare.

By midafternoon he wobbily hauled himself up a rusty iron ladder at Meigs Field, the island airport. He slumped to the very warm cement facedown to absorb some heat for his cold body. It was only minutes before he looked up and saw a security car with flashing lights headed toward him. It stopped with the front tires not that far from his head. He heard a voice.

"Are you dead?"

"Apparently not," he answered. "I swam down from Muskegon in the last couple days."

"Oh bullshit!"

"Okay, I walked on water!"

"You can't nap here. This is an airport."

"I'm looking for a room to rent."

"Here?"

"In Chicago. A few blocks from the beach."

"My sister's got a spare room up on Astor. A little expensive. For gentlemen only. You're not a faggot?"

"Apparently not. Isn't that impolite?"

"Sorry. The room is forty dollars a week."

"That's doable." Thad was thinking of the wad of cash Frank had passed him plus he had been saving for a trip to see the Pacific Ocean.

He felt more than a tinge of anxiety getting up from the warm secure cement. Why couldn't he stay there? His father had made much of his minimal ambitions: wanting to swim in the Pacific, planning to swim around Manhattan Island, Japan to the mainland, Havana to Key West, a project which others had failed at. But just why was he here other than the wonderful water between where he was up in Michigan and Chicago? He could not dismiss the hollowness in his stomach that stood for timidity or even fear. Chicago looked too large and unpleasant, much more so than Washington, D.C., or New York City both of which he had hitchhiked to the year before just to see what they looked like in *real life,* including the hole in the ground that was 9/11. He had long since recognized the wide stretch of sheer daffiness in his own character, including what his father called "tempting fate." He could have called Laurie rather than making the forbidden stop while swimming. Frank had warned him that he would "kick his ass" if he tried to visit Laurie who would have met him anywhere. He had his *jaw* to pay for that stupidity.

He slipped on trousers and a shirt from his fanny pack and off he went to look for a room halfway across town with the security officer named Bud thinking of his water babies back home. Did they need his protection? Did he need his own protection? Probably. The Astor neighborhood looked too expensive but the house was splendid with a big flower garden in the backyard. The meeting went well with a load of eccentric rules. No girls in the room unless related or you're at least engaged. No hot plates. Coffeepot always going in kitchen. Any help in yard deducted from rent. She was a hefty woman who said he was a "cutie." Lake Michigan was only a few blocks to the north. Her name was Willa and she had a slightly Irish accent. He paid several weeks ahead and when asked said he had no luggage because he had swum down from Muskegon. Her eyes widened and she said a distant cousin had swum the English Channel and had won an Olympic medal. His room had an outside door to the garden. He said good-bye and thank you to Bud then dozed on the spacious bed while reading a typed sheet which held the closest restaurants and places of *worship*. He still felt a specific hollowness in his stomach and brooded about both Laurie and Emily. He was going to have to bite the bullet and buy his first cell phone. He was the only one his age, seventeen, who didn't have one. This was a matter of pride and snobbery and wanting to save what money he earned for his future dreams. But now for reasons of loneliness he wanted to call both Emily and Laurie and he owed his mother a call of explanation. She was used to disappearances of a couple of days but this was pushing it. And who knows what problems Frank would cause. He had looked at the inception of the cell phone like his father had that of the Hula-Hoop and the Frisbee.

He took a shower and then a walk toward the business district. He bought a couple of Chicago Cubs T-shirts and then, feeling intimidated, walked into a cell phone store. However there was a pleasant young Mexican girl who walked him through the paces and he bought the simplest prepaid model with a hundred minutes, walked down the street, and sat on a park bench. First was Mother who was pissed off when he said he was in Chicago. She said she needed help on the farm because his father had gone on a rampage. Someone had slashed his tires at the tavern and he suspected it was Friendly Frank's crew of mechanics. He said lamely, "I can't stay there forever, I have to seek my fortune," at which point she hung up. He then called Laurie which began unsatisfactorily because both she and her father were in the kitchen and she pretended she was talking to her friend Lisa. He said he was okay but also told her the tire-slashing story and she said, "Shit, that's awful" and yelled it out to her dad who escaped the kitchen. They were at a dead end so he hung up and called Emily who said that her father wanted to meet him. He could get Thad a job. They could have breakfast at the Drake tomorrow which was near his office. She had told him that her father had grown up on a big farm in eastern Kansas. Thad could see the Drake in the distance so stopped in a clothing store and bought a lightweight summer sport coat for a modest price. Emily was working for her father for the summer so they agreed to meet at 5 p.m.

Thad was now in a bit of a turmoil. There is an easy-going arrogance in seventeen-year-olds. They are either absurdly self-confident or involved in a withered state of mind. Now Thad was in between. He was out in the world wisely out of range of Friendly Frank and seeing what the actual world looked like, albeit a little bit prematurely. There was a bit of tentative trembling, the shuddering elevator that life presents without quite enough emotional scar tissue to solidify him. There was an unimaginable number of people on the streets which did not have a calming influence. The feeling was similar to the collective sensations between late fall and early spring when he couldn't swim because of the cold. He'd spend days walking up and down the river staring at it, enjoying the families of otters he saw occasionally with their crazy chatter and squeaks and their great speed in the water.

Now on the park bench he wondered if all water babies were born in spring because they certainly couldn't endure midwinter. He was furious at Frank for driving him from the sacred place which he had to return to or die trying which was not out of the question. He sat there mute and a little despondent before the vast sweep of traffic, human and vehicular, the broad snake of cars heading north to where Emily lived. What was he doing here? Good question. He suddenly felt as if he was watching a goofy rerun of *Twilight Zone* which his father liked but he largely ignored. Who else among this man swarm had seen a water baby much less touched one lightly? He supposed that this somehow set him apart. Should he have stayed with them or was he justified in having fled? Perhaps this race of creatures had lasted forever and was good at it. He had never believed in ghosts, spirits, God or gods, except what Tooth had told him and they seemed to belong to her people. Once as a boy he had camped some after Tooth's teenage daughter had died in an auto accident with a drunk boy. All night in her dreams Tooth called out to her daughter in the tent. It had been raining lightly and at dawn Thad, who was only ten at the time, was sure he had seen Tooth's daughter standing out in the rain staring at him through the open tent flap. He told Tooth and she wailed and wailed singing her daughter's death song. Another strange thing happened when he was thirteen and hunting ruffed grouse to eat with a friend. The friend who was a nitwit shot a large male raven with a shotgun. The raven fell wounded in the river and Thad thought it was staring at him accusatorily so he impulsively dove in the river and retrieved it. He held the raven in his arms until it shuddered into death, and he had also shuddered as it stared at him until it died. He told his friend never to mention the matter under the threat of pain. Thad's dog Mutt was used to digging holes for dead creatures he found and dug a hole for the raven. Tooth claimed that the souls of dead infants entered birds and maybe the raven had entered him? He only saw its eyes when he was swimming far underwater. Thad was the ace junior naturalist of the school system and his oldest and best teacher had advised him not to say things were impossible in a universe with ninety billion galaxies. Einstein had said that it's not for scientists to drill holes in a thin piece of board. All mysteries must be explored. Thad loved to read about the inconceivability of some bird migrations. One altruistic species flew twelve thousand miles without stopping. His mother thought the greatest human miracle was Mozart, about which he had no opinion. He preferred the outside and a warbler that landed on his knee in May while he was sitting, perhaps back from the Bahamas to northern Michigan.

He sat there in his own alien stiffness and felt an itch to swim on seeing the blue lakeshore in the distance but then it was time to meet Emily. Still a block away, he could see her under the Drake's canopy talking to a bellhop among the sparse arriving cabs and limos. When he reached them she turned with delight.

"Lee, this is Thad. Help him out if he needs it but don't introduce him to any women. He's mine."

"Of course, Emily."

Thad felt like a clod, an ungainly farm boy, walking past the immense arrangement of flowers in the lobby of the Drake and into the elegant elevator. "Dad keeps these rooms for business reasons," Emily said as if no one else were in the elevator. "Mom thinks otherwise." She laughed. "Her ancestors were Boston Puritans which means they traded in spices, whales, and slaves. Her nose is so sharp you could cut yourself on it. Her relatives went to Harvard and Yale and Dad went to Kansas State." When they entered the moderately large suite Emily threw herself on the big bed, opened her legs, and beckoned him.

"Not in your father's room," he said.

"Chicken shit," she hissed, "then where?" She got up and went to the living room and took little opera glasses from her purse and aimed them at the street. "Look, he's standing by the door talking to a politician we support. We bought him a fucking Escalade." He was standing right behind her and she wiggled her butt into his crotch which he couldn't resist and he lifted the skirt of her business suit and she pulled down her panties. In like Flynn, there was a knock on the door and a voice calling "room service." He was out, her skirt fell, and the door opened.

"A snack your dad sent up," a black waiter announced, "a white burgundy and lump crabmeat, your favorite, and your dad's bourbon. He'll be up shortly."

"Thanks, Harold," Emily said touching his arm.

Harold glanced at Thad with a trace of "you lucky white prick" and left.

Emily quickly bent over the sofa so they could finish. Thad felt pleased but jangled. He had intermittently been thinking of his grandpa and a curious deathbed scene where he and his mother sat up all night as Grandpa was fading. His old friend the country doctor had been there a couple hours the evening before but then Tooth took him back across the river. When Tooth returned she sat in a straight-back chair against the wall near Grandpa's head. Everyone knew they had been lovers for years. A half dozen miles east into the woods Grandpa and Tooth had a deer hunting cabin. They waited for snow in mid-November and hauled the meat onto a toboggan. The doctor had left in the evening when Grandpa had said, "Please let me go." His heart was fluttery like a wounded sparrow's and he thought such panic was inappropriate for one saying farewell to the beautiful earth. From his windows he saw the frost-yellowed willows bordering the river. He told Thad over and over, also his mother, not to spend their lives working as hard as he had. Like his father Thaddeus, Grandpa felt that twelve hours was a proper workday, longer in the summer when the available light would allow it. He was a gnarled mass of arthritic muscle known all his life for his strength as certain men are in rural areas where such talent is of actual value. Grandpa was the only member of the family who was all-out enthused by Thad's swimming and they also fly-fished for brown trout in the river a great deal. For his parents Thad was expected to go to a nearby lake for wonderful-eating perch and bluegills which his parents preferred over trout.

Thad sat there on the sofa in the suite rather glumly nibbling on the crabmeat and sipping the wines which were both delicious, a tad depleted from the sex, but reviving as Emily showed him a tiny incision scar from a knee operation. Her skin was slightly olive because she said she had been adopted from a Chicago Italian from Friuli. His glumness came from the idea that the suite must cost as much or much more than their farm must make in a day but then he had read so much about the financial misbalance of the culture he was nauseated. Obviously the suite cost more than the farm made in a day despite their brutally hard work.

He slid back into his consciousness, his hand on Emily's. He was spooked by the fundamental change in his view of life made by seeing the water babies sipping the polliwogs in the pond. The world, simply enough, wasn't the same place it had been previous to that date.

"A penny for your thoughts," Emily said refilling his wineglass when he could have used the glass of bourbon waiting for her father, he was that disjointed.

"When I was little, before kindergarten, I wore a leather harness so I wouldn't drown in a little spring pond behind the farmhouse. One day Grandpa became superstitious when he saw me cuddled with a baby beaver in the grass near some cattails with the ordinarily wary mother beaver swimming by close to her child unconcerned. Tooth calmed Grandpa down saying it wasn't that odd while Grandpa worried that they were losing his grandson to the animal world. A few months later when my mother was picking blackberries for jam she saw little me walking along the riverbank with a bear and stopping to roll and wrestle followed by the big sow mother. My mother shrieked in fear and then the she-cub alarmed rolled down the bank into the river. I went in after it and handed it back wet. The sow nipped me for carelessness growling in anger. I swam across the river to my mother who had wondered why my pant legs had been torn lately. Playing with a bear cub Grandpa was worried about the sow but knew if he shot it the cub would die in the coming winter. Tooth said leave them all alone. She had made friends with a cub and they were still friends fourteen years later. A bear will let you know when it's pissed by its eyes and a growl. You don't approach them, you let them approach you. Creatures want companionship but on their own terms so I was warned rather than forbidden contact."

Emily was delighted saying that she always had wanted a part animal for a boyfriend. A key turned and her father entered.

"I should have knocked."

"Why?" Emily said teasingly.

"Yes of course my virgin sister of mercy in your black BMW." He shook Thad's hand. "You're a chesty lad. Farm raised, I understand, so am I."

"Yes, sir." Thad shook his hand thinking he had never seen such a beautiful suit. He had two first names: John Scott Walpole.

They chatted about their mutual farm background with John Scott being raised on a large soybean and wheat operation in eastern Kansas and with Brazil getting the edge on soybeans right now it was all wheat, run by his two brothers and what with great wheat prices now the timing was perfect. John Scott insisted that Thad get his cheek checked before he began work for him at a warehouse and Thad said he had a doctor's number.

"Then do it." John Scott inanely handed him the phone.

At that moment Emily walked to the corner as Thad's cell rang and she looked at the caller ID. She picked up and listened a moment then shrieked and slid down with her butt on the floor. Thad ran to her and took the phone and quickly dizzied and wilted himself. Thad's father had gone to a farm auction down the road and been beaten with tire irons by three of Friendly Frank's mechanics that morning. He was now in the ICU at Grand Rapids Blodget. Now John Scott took the phone. It is not widely known how effective and energetic some men of wealth and power (third-generation Chicago commercial real estate) are. Within minutes he talked to Rick, Thad's mother, Frank's daughter Laurie, a Northwestern University classmate who was thought to be a lawyer and the hardest piece of work in Grand Rapids, the Kent County prosecutor and the Kent County sheriff, ending with "Just be there," his functional King Air pilot at Meigs, called his driver, ordered sandwiches to pack along, then explained how they were going to *clarify* matters. He was totally conscious that this wasn't his business but it defiled his sense of order and his daughter's well-being. On the way to the airport Thad continued to fill him in on the past events to which he responded "I hate bullies" and "small town big shots" recounting a couple of major rural Kansas friends. In two hours they were in Thad's father's hospital room at Blodgett along with the prosecutor, sheriff, and John Scott's lawyer. Thad kissed his father's forehead. He was in a half-body and head cast.

"I hope you're stupid enough to testify that our client started a fight with three big men with tire irons?" the lawyer said to the sheriff.

Thad felt uncomfortable. His favorite teacher taught history and was known locally as the "left winger" but was also the best fisherman and hunter which got him off the political hook locally. His notion was that the human beast's knack for unnecessarily crushing each other kept the human race on the hot seat. He contended that he had been treated more politely in a North Vietnam prison camp than by the local Republicans. He had amassed a great deal of historical knowledge about the violence of language and now in the hospital room it seemed meaningless to Thad to wipe up the floor with the sheriff when the central malefactor was Friendly Frank who would finally be charged for the barrel stave across the cheek and his own daughter would testify. Laurie had told him that her father had been deeply embarrassed when the police had explained that it was Thad who had saved him from hypothermia and drowning. Laurie wanted Thad to sue her father for enough to go out to Scripps in California, his heart's desire, which was to study water and its inhabitants. He was pleased that Emily's father John Scott was on their side but was lucidly aware that he was the kind of man of immense wealth and power who had made the world financial community such a mess in recent times. As his teacher had drummed into them, how could greed be the primary virtue of a culture?

The sheriff had been squeezed dry and feeble.

"I'm surprised that you're unconcerned

by the violence in your territory. Look at this young man's face."

"He was trespassing," the sheriff said lamely.

"He was on the dock at the invitation of the daughter, his classmate. That cannot be construed as trespassing any more than shooting someone trick-or-treating on Halloween. No citizen has that kind of freedom any more than he has owning a pit bull that kills a neighbor's kid. Your Friendly Frank is not all in all a bad guy, is publicly generous, but should not be allowed to control the community as a bully."

"He's not going to be allowed to," said John Scott. "He's about to get his ass kicked."

That's where Thad felt uncomfortable. It wasn't the battle of the titans but maybe the battle of dicks. Why did men have to be this way? Thad's doubt from Chicago reentered him. Emily was holding his father's head and flirting with him.

"You're prettier than a speckled pup," she said.

"We say that in Kansas," John Scott added, proud of his daughter's beauty.

The hospital room became inconclusive except the sheriff was humiliated and the prosecutor angry with him. "You've got to stop sucking up to Friendly Frank. Look at the boy's face. That's clearly felonious assault. And now look at his father for Christ's sake. You're letting a bully run the town. I know he was your largest campaign contributor."

Thad felt a slight wave of nausea over money and power, including Laurie and Emily. Nothing ever seemed to be denied to rich girls. He met Laurie in Grand Rapids last fall for her school shopping and a Chinese meal and a trip to Schuler Books and he had estimated she had spent a couple of grand which seemed repellent. What kind of preparation for life can wealth be except to make it easy? At least Emily and Laurie had a lot of curiosity and were good students. In the seventh grade his crush was Tooth's niece. They hung out camping, fishing, and hunting. Everyone called her Dove because doves weren't legal hunting prey in Michigan, a law she always violated. She shot them with her BB gun or baited and trapped them, plucked them and gutted them over a wood fire for Thad. Her father was the prime somewhat legal tribal meat supplier, shooting as many as thirty deer in the fall for older members. Sometimes when they camped and fished for brown trout Dove would cook a stew of

194

dried sweet corn, venison, and fresh squash. They had such a good time his heart broke apart when they split up and she said, "You like those rich pretty cunts not a big-nosed Chip girl."

It was obvious Dove was going to go fast as a wife because of her hunting and cooking abilities. Now she had two kids and when she came out to the farm it was a melancholy occasion. Dove frequently irritated his father because she always outfished him. When they'd go off on a fishing trip in a rowboat they'd pack along a Dutch oven and her renowned store of sundried sweet corn, wild leeks, squash, and venison including many marrow bones. It was Thad's favorite dish in life. He even liked Dove's husband, a gentle and kind soul with no drinking problems. He felt strangely jealous of the children age two and three, a girl and a boy, named Pudge and Bone, who behaved like bear cubs. Thad himself was known among the tribal people as Human Fish. Tooth told him that a northern Michigan writer friendly with the tribe and author of somber works was known as One Who Goes into the Dark a Long Ways and We Hope He Comes Back. Generally in America tribal people are desperately misunderstood because no one takes the trouble and aggressive snoops are not welcome. Rather than dream, white people are given more latitude just as earlier in our history exploratory botanists were revered as *earth divers.* Thad was never sure what to think, having grown up around them so he had never felt distanced. There was nothing particularly spiritual about it but was mostly Grandpa's matter-of-fact English *at home* sense of where he lived.

When they all left the hospital room there was a general sense of victory except with Thad, who as a *peacemaker* just wanted it to be over and had invoked his water babies in his head to calm himself down. He remembered with amusement when he and Dove would push the rowboat off to go camping Tooth would call from the porch "No babies, please," and he would be embarrassed and Dove would laugh and shove.

Emily and John Scott had dinner at the farm and spent the night. They loved the little dragline barge that got them to the island. "I feel safe here," said John Scott and Thad wondered why he ever felt unsafe owning a goodly piece of Chicago. Thad's mother had some Cornish pasties in her freezer. Both her grandmother and John Scott's people were from the Lyme Regis area of Cornwall and there was a good evening of chatter but about 3 a.m. the bottom fell out of the family. Dove called saying the state police came to the door saying her husband had died in an auto accident near Mount Pleasant on the way back from a meeting in Lansing, the state capital, on tribal business. Tooth began to wail with power and she and Thad's mother drove off to pick up Dove and the babies as Dove didn't like her in-laws. They were back in an hour and John Scott sat on the sofa between Tooth and her niece both of whom were wailing at a volume never used in the funerals or mourning of white people. Dove kept screaming what would happen to the babies and her. Thad's mother shushed her and she and Tooth took her to the spare bedroom near the pump house on the main floor. They would clear it all, it was a big room, and Dove and her babies would move in with them after they enclosed a bathroom. Dove could help with the farm while Thad's father convalesced. Emily piped up that babies needed a father figure and Thad would work. "The dreamer?" Dove asked and everyone laughed. It was an obvious relief to Dove and Tooth that they would be taken in partly because of Dove's dislike for her in-laws. Thad liked the idea of playing

Dad to the two roly-polies while working on the farm. Meanwhile he and John Scott were making breakfast for everyone. John Scott said that as the sixth son and no daughter on the farm he had to help his mother with the cooking and learned to enjoy it. It was pleasant setting up a pork roast for lunch rather than freezing your ass in October. Making bread and rolls was his favorite. Emily was in the way and couldn't crack an egg so formed sausage patties. Dove pushed Thad aside to make some big cheese omelets and he held the babies fighting on his lap on the sofa. They were laughing and trying to bite each other. He had always wanted a sister but now could see how combative they could be. Even though they were the same size she was the better fighter, as with lions.

By breakfast time and a big skillet of fried new potatoes Dove was pacified, with a nice place to live among people she loved including her aunt. Children sense that grandmothers are substitute mothers and the babies were easily controlled by Tooth where Thad struggled.

Thad and John Scott went out to the front porch to stare at the river, the only possible palliative. John Scott lightly brought up the idea that Thad might need financing.

"That might be inappropriate," Thad said. "Since Great-Grandpa we've been proud we kept our heads above water here."

"What about college for instance. It's up to thirty or forty grand a year. I'm putting what was Emily's soccer team through college. We recruited them from third world areas in Chicago. Faster and hungrier."

"Maybe I'll get a scholarship to a good place."

"And maybe not."

"Well marine biology and oceanography weren't the most rational choices but what I love."

"You're Emily's friend. And in a religious sense I tithe to education because it's what I believe in and I can afford it. Just think of members of Congress being truly educated."

"I can't imagine." Thad laughed. He had been quietly brooding about tomorrow being Tomato Day, June 4, the first date felt to be guaranteed frost free.

Thad had looked at the two hundred 5-foot-long hardwood stakes in storage. He hoped to start at 5 a.m. to finish in one day. Laurie wanted to come out to help as she had the two previous years. She and her mother flower gardened at home but her father felt that growing vegetables was low-class and ugly. Mother was going to pick up Dad at the Grand Rapids hospital in the morning. She had been worried about the cost but the lawyer said that could be an easy lawsuit. John Scott dozed off. He would be picked up for his plane to Chicago in a few hours so they would have an early supper that Dove and Tooth were working on. Thad glanced at the sleeping John Scott and wondered how though everyone in the culture seemed to want to be wealthy it couldn't be easy if you also had a conscience. How could you help if that were possible? It seemed apparent in the recent press that men such as Warren Buffett and Bill Gates actually seemed disturbed about extreme wealth.

Emily came tiptoeing down the path in a tiny swimsuit for a dip in the river. It was unreasonably warm for early June and she swatted a mosquito on her arm. Thad's thoughts were errant. It was somehow the twin mysteries of sexual attraction and the water babies he had seen. Was it wrong to keep their beauty from those he loved? Probably. Laurie's life was so blemished by her horrid father. By coincidence his cell rang and it said Laurie so he answered but it was her father who began ranting immediately saying that if his daughter testified against him he would disown her, thus Thad would cost his only child millions of dollars. Thad joked that it would be good for her to work for a living. Friendly Frank went berserk saying that if Thad didn't drop charges, also his dad, they were in grave danger. Thad said he would be glad to pass along his threat to the prosecutor. The man started yelling, then there was a shriek. Laurie grabbed the phone from her father and ran for it, saying she hoped to get out that evening after her father's monthly special *gourmet dinner.* She couldn't leave her mother alone without defense as her father tended to be especially impetuous during these dinners when the menu was composed of things the dozen invitees brought. The cook was a graduate student at the University of Michigan and from Lyon, France, who had a part-time business catering such meals for rich Americans.

Thad disrobed to his undies and swam with Emily to keep her safe as the current was swift on the river's far side. There was a hollow in a bank thicket so they could neck in privacy and more. Emily was strong from sports but didn't look so with a smooth body. He felt it was more likely he'd show Laurie the water babies. Laurie had spent time growing up in the largest woodlot behind their house to avoid her parents and as a student of nature would find the water babies less alarming.

Tooth and Dove had made a venison stew for supper that John Scott thought tasted French. Tooth explained that many Chippewas had married French Canadians, including her grandmother who married a man from Montreal who worked in the timber business. She had gone to France once and loved to tell tribal members how the French ate snakes which were really eels.

Emily begged to stay behind to help with the tomato planting. She loved tomatoes but had no real idea how they were raised. Thad assured John Scott he would be back in Chicago after things calmed down. John Scott said that Emily would rent a car and they could drive down the coast, or even through the Upper Peninsula and down through Wisconsin. He explained he had owned a nice little farm way up near Ladysmith, Wisconsin, but had a *flirtation* with a woman who pursued him to Chicago and in order to save his marriage he sold the farm.

Pudge and Bone were making trouble fighting and biting each other and Dove and Tooth were played out cleaning up after dinner. Thad's mother had gone to her room over worry about her wounded husband. Pudge and Bone had never had a proper naming ceremony. Pudge was almost three and ate too much but was very tough and Bone nearly four, named by Tooth for his propensity for toying with his pecker which little boys do. They felt the vacuum of their father's death. What can little children know about death? Thad tried to take care of the kids and repeatedly read them *Goodnight Moon,* one of his favorite stories. They dozed off in their big bed in the new quarters organized for them by Thad's mother. Thad went back to his current book *Fluvial Processes in Geomorphology,* a primer text for water people. June is hard on children because bedtime isn't dark that close to the solstice so they think it's unfair they should be in bed when there's still daylight. When John Scott and the plane had buzzed the farm twice Bone had yelled "Bird" and Pudge screamed "Plane," jumping Bone's back, bearing him to the ground and punching him. She clearly saw herself as her brother's cop, the queen of earthly order.

About half past ten he heard Laurie yelling from across the river. He fetched her in the rowboat and it was a grim story. Thad, his mother, Emily, Dove, Tooth sat with her at the kitchen table. During the dessert course of the fancy dinner Friendly Frank's nasty lawyer had started goading Laurie about testifying against her father. She said, "Don't talk to me." Her father had crammed the soufflé in her face, breaking her nose with the pan. Everyone left in disgust except the lawyer, naturally. Laurie's eyes were black and blue.

"You should have let him drown," Thad's mother said.

"Next deer season I'll shoot the cocksucker," Tooth offered. "I know where he hunts."

Emily held the trembling Laurie and Thad brooded while his mother had a much needed drink. He felt both murderous and powerless. He would make sure the prosecutor learned what had happened to a witness.

Thad was up at 4 a.m. having coffee in the first trace of light on the eastern-facing front porch. He heard the tractor and went to help his mother load the flats of tomato plants onto the wagon next to her greenhouse where she had started them out in early May. Dove brought him out an egg sandwich which he ate hastily, then began driving the two hundred stakes. The process was simple in that you attached the planted tomato to the stake with a twist tie of the kind used to seal a loaf of bread. He felt good about the oncoming day. Many are ignorant of the fact that hard manual labor can make you feel good though he thought that nothing topped a fine hour swim. There was a little dread over the predicted ninety-degree weather but Mother said they'd quit at noon and finish tomorrow. Dove would make them a picnic and they would walk upstream to the pond where the water babies lived. He had decided that anyone on his tomato crew had to be considered trustworthy. Meanwhile he felt in his stomach the mystery of sexuality. He had given Emily and Laurie his bed and slept tilted way back in the La-Z-Boy reading chair. When he awoke and turned on a small light they were in a knot under a sheet with Emily's hand on Laurie whose face was considerably more bloated, reminding him of his own after her father had hit him. This man was inexplicably violent even with those he purportedly loved. The sheet was twisted halfway up their bodies and still in half sleep the vision was electrifying and then mixed in with his need to see his water babies that afternoon, another mystery he couldn't simplify. He was distracted by an early fantasy about swimming around Manhattan Island. He had recently checked the water current and it struck him as a simple feat.

Nearly all of his swimming was done in near-wilderness conditions and he liked the idea of swimming past immense buildings and millions of people. As a student of the natural world he did not ignore the works of man who in his view was nature too, so said Shakespeare who also seemed a mystery to Thad along with his mother's Mozart addiction.

He worked hard and quickly in the heat of the morning, streaming sweat, and occasionally his mother would spray him down with insect repellent. Mosquitoes loved still, humid mornings, and their steady whine was obnoxious. He mostly held the stakes as he drove them in. The rest of the crew showed up sleepily at 8 a.m. and they were off and running. How beautiful he thought to think of red ripe tomatoes as the future of their work. They'd sell a hundred bushels to the town women who still liked to can their own tomatoes in rows of Ball jars.

By 11 a.m. they were half done and decided to surge on, skipping lunch in favor of a midafternoon picnic though they broke for a quick refreshing swim. Rather than looking at Emily and Laurie he consoled himself with thinking about stories his mother had told him about the great cities she had visited, London, Paris, and New York, with him chiming in questions about the swimming possibilities of the Thames, Seine, and Hudson. When told these rivers were filthy he wasn't troubled because mothers were always cautionary and he had swum in many muddy rivers. He decided swimming these three rivers would put order in his life, adding the great rivers of the American West. He might have to wait as his life savings was less than three thousand dollars. Of course he was aware that if he captured and sold a water baby everything would be possible but this would be akin to Judas and the crucifixion. This notion brought immediate despondency similar to the slump of March and April. It was bad enough not to be able to swim but to also be unable to have the substitute exertion of cross-country skiing brought on a particular despondency as the snows melted and he could no longer glide through the hills and forest. Some people have to burn up or become smudge. Hate can become a trigger and when he looked at Laurie his burgeoning hate for her father brought on an exhaustion. Surely part of the greatest evil of evil men is that they make you hate them.

Right now in the early afternoon he was

concocting murder plots. Late in the summer he would often see Friendly Frank brown trout fishing with a guide. There were open areas on the river and the fields produced thousands of grasshoppers, which brown trout fed on with gusto when the hoppers landed in the river. Many took advantage of this phenomenon and Thad concocted an idea where he would hide behind a larger boulder above a rapid and when the guide came through with Friendly Frank he would swim underwater after them, and when they reached the right place he would set his feet on the bottom and tip over his boat. By fish and game law the guide always wore a life preserver, but not Friendly Frank who was above all law. The guide would be fine but within a day Friendly Frank would have a severe case of the bloat.

He felt heartsick and queasy from his murder fantasy. What right did he have to kill anyone? He was nearly done with the stakes and Mother was off to pick up Dad in the hospital in Grand Rapids and would be back in an hour. Laurie would manage the tomato crew. Thad scooped up Pudge and Bone who were being pains in the ass. Bone had decided to repeatedly scream, "I want my daddy." He headed upriver toward the water baby pond. Emily followed, relieving him of the burden of Bone after a few hundred yards. Pudge immediately captured a small garter snake with which she tormented her brother who was phobic about snakes. He wept piteously. Thad pitched the snake in the nearby river at which Pudge screamed having lost her pet.

"This is the downside of child rearing," Emily said. "I'll still want a baby if you want one."

"We'll wait until I have a livelihood."

"You're such a prick. It's not my fault if I have some money. I was born that way."

"I'm sorry. I don't want your money, I want your ass."

"How about now?"

The kids were well in front of them on the trail and Emily detoured behind a huge maple for a stand-up quickie.

This was not the most satisfying form of lovemaking and he stumbled backward into the wide growth with Emily glancing with amusement at him on the ground.

At the pond Thad quickly stepped out of his clothes and entered the pond fearing the water babies may have escaped into the river but there they were, perhaps a dozen in all in the deepest part of the pond drifting in a shaft of sunlight and watching his slow approach. Emily followed him but turned in sudden alarm and thrashed away in seeing them. He held out his hands and one curled up in his palms. He held it up for Pudge and Bone to see. Bone bellowed in horror, but Pudge shrieked with delight petting it. Thad replaced the water baby with the others and got out of the pond. Emily was pale and looked at him questioningly.

"It's my secret," he said. "They're water babies like in the old story. Tooth said they develop from the souls of dead infants."

"I'm not sure I can take it," Emily said.

Pudge threw herself into the water and Thad went after her. He knew she could swim but he had never seen her deep underwater. There she was in the circle of water babies who petted this miniature human as if she were a puppy. At this point he decided that at picnic time he wouldn't show anyone else but perhaps bring Laurie out in the next few days. She certainly deserved this splendid diversion. Rather than further murderous thoughts he had to depend on Friendly Frank being ruined legally. Emily's cell rang and they were beckoned back to the farmhouse for the picnic because his mother had returned with his dad who was still unable to walk this far downriver.

■ ■ ■ ■

PART II

■ ■ ■ ■

Thad and Emily stayed another ten days then rented a car for Chicago, not wanting to ride in John Scott's plane but preferring a slow trip. Thad would be obligated to return in August. The X-rays to be used for evidence had revealed a dozen small fractures in his cheekbone. The doctor had said, "The pain must have been awful," to which Thad replied simply, "It was." At the picnic table Thad's father had been overwhelmed to see Laurie's black eyes. Tooth patted his hand and announced loudly, "I'm going to shoot the son of a bitch with my 30.06 this coming deer season. Enough is enough," to which no one responded. "I'll pop his head off. This is called damage control."

Thad had been chewing on his wonderful fried chicken thinking that humans are ill-prepared for the miraculous. It's too much of a jolt and the human soul is not spacious enough to deal with it. What happens when we sense and see the eternal in the ordinary present? What should he do about the water babies? Absolutely nothing. The idea that wild creatures always need our help was repugnant to him. He would look at them again at the time of the court case in August. Meanwhile he had to resume some sort of equilibrium connected to day-to-day life. Oddly they were passing Ludington, a lovely city by the sea on Lake Michigan which always temporarily knocked him off his pins. A dear friend had lived here whom he knew because they were both half-milers at different high schools. They usually finished in a virtual dead heat including the state finals when his friend won by a footfall. A week later he had been swept from the Ludington Pier and drawn to his death by an undertow. Throughout the Great Lakes boys and young men race huge waves sometimes successfully.

He told Emily the story and she was upset by the freakish nature of challenging waves. Was it to show your courage? Not having grown up on the coast Thad wasn't sure. There were dozens of examples of foolhardy behavior. He recalled a mountaineering guide calling his children from the top of Everest by cell phone to say that Dad wasn't going to make it home. The least comprehensible to Thad was race car driving that killed so many. Swimming was fast enough to him, though the drowning rate was not negligible.

Emily brought up religion and they tried to keep it light. Her grandmother had been a radical Evangelical which had somewhat traumatized her father who viewed monotheism as one of the world's great ills in terms of war and sheer murder. Thad said that his parents allowed Tooth to take him to Sunday school. She had grown up on an Ontario reservation run by an Episcopalian missionary and thought the Resurrection was a *great idea,* while his mother was agnostic but a strict ethicist.

He himself was quite spiritual in an eccentric way based on all of his reading in the life sciences and astronomy wherein everything seemed to be too monstrously intricate to be accidental whether it was avian vision and migration or the sheer fact of ninety billion galaxies. One could scarcely be cynical about this despite the absurd behavior of Evangelicals and Mormons or the history of the Catholic Church, the minimalization of a *moral* life. A history teacher he mourned who had been fired for too many DUIs said that a common thread of genius ran through Mozart, Caravaggio, and Gauguin that was divine whatever that in itself meant. He felt that our culture's general instruction manual was enough to puke a maggot. He had learned early not to try to formalize his interesting perceptions or they would stagnate. All of this certainly was not enough to pass for religion but he didn't care partly because he was still young. His first love, swimming, was certainly not eternal but then so was earth and any creature, human or otherwise.

While they talked Emily's face was knotted in puzzlement. She had talked several times in their quiet moments about the six months she had worked at an orphanage managed by a cousin in the unfashionable southern border of Kenya. She loved taking care of the children and teaching them to read. It was a wonderful time several years back before she enrolled in Sarah Lawrence when she was taking a year off from *learning.* She felt *fulfilled* by her work.

Disaster hit when both Emily's cousin and her black boyfriend had died of AIDS this spring and any faint idea that Emily might want to return to Africa drove her father to the edge of berserk. Emily could clearly see that her father's enthusiasm for Thad as her love interest came clearly from this fear of Africa. This all became twisted in Thad's mind with the death of his Ludington friend and the eerie feeling he had as one of the six pallbearers carrying the casket from the Methodist church. Not oddly it filled him with the urgency to get on with his own life. This desperation of mortality is always present when someone close dies, even Dove's husband. His brain seemed a little bruised by too much happening in recent months. He had the opposite of a soldier's mentality in that anything akin to violence repelled him, even talking about it. To the disgust of his high school's football coach he had refused to take part but the coach wanted his track speed and strength. He held the school record time for the hand-over-hand rope climb, going up the large rope that hung from the gym ceiling. You didn't use your legs just arms and shoulders. But then he recognized that coaches are interested in coaches and careers that are enhanced by the strong and fast. He told Emily about the most important event of his life which occurred when he was eight. He had driven to Texas, flying was too expensive, with his parents for a family reunion of his father's people. One day in East Texas they wandered around Larry McMurtry's famed used bookstore and he spotted a huge book published in England

called *The Rivers of Earth.* He was dumb-
founded with curiosity and his parents after
a quarrel bought it for him. Thad was
forever grateful to his mother to insist on
his having the book. His mother insisted
that it was hard enough to be a boy on a
remote farm but he shouldn't have to go
without good books. She visited the library
once a week and Thad usually went with
her. Once the very homely librarian came
out for Sunday lunch and announced that
she had fatal pancreatic cancer. She didn't
mind dying she said although a male had
never kissed her. Thad's father at the table
grabbed her and kissed her violently then
wept. For inexplicable reasons they all
laughed. His mother pushed him into reading Emily Brontë, Sherwood Anderson, and
Dostoyevsky, certainly a mixed bag with a
sheer tonnage of emotions that drove Thad
frequently to the river. After lunch that day
in which the adults drank too much cheap
California wine Thad went out to the porch
and the librarian followed. He shed his
clothes down to his skivvies for a swim. He
heard her say, "You have a nice physique"
and his throat closed up. How could he be
embarrassed underwater but he was. He
held his breath as long as possible until well
downstream. He recalled his father warning

him not to become too soft but then felt he wouldn't become too soft if everyone else was too hard. The general cruelty of life was too often overwhelming. Why wasn't the librarian a trace more attractive? What was the evolutionary purpose of homeliness in this otherwise delightful person? How can one give up these relentless questions? Two years in a row he had taken a girl to the prom because no one else would.

Back to his dad saying you can't accept anything as it is presented to you. You have to question the nature of everything. Though young both Emily and Laurie seemed bent on permanent coupling but he was mindful of how often both male and females in his high school class seemed to change their minds. Even his mother had seemed a bit sweet on the Finnish bachelor farmer a few miles downriver. For himself it made more sense to take up with Dove because her children needed a father. It was his understanding that it was how it was done in groups in the old days. The group was more important than free choice in love. Tooth wanted her daughter to take up with an older Indian farmer who owned a lot of property in the northern part of the county about thirty miles away. Tooth was interested in the financial survival of Dove's children more than the happiness of her niece whom she viewed as not born to be happy. This wasn't a judgment of Dove but just the nature of her character. Thad had always been puzzled about the sides of his own character. One half wanted to simply stay home and grow from a farm boy to a farm man, but the other half was a water obsessive who had been wearing out the book *The Rivers of Earth* for a decade, and had studied maps of all the great cities of Earth that he could likely navigate: Hong Kong, Calcutta, New York City, and Los Angeles as well as his hometown. He thought it was wonderful that John Scott wanted to help him with college but ultimately he was afraid that with help would come control. People wanted to help you do what they wanted you to do and both Laurie and Emily wanted to pin him down to be their very own. It reminded him of his refusal to pin butterflies for biology class. He only wanted to see butterflies flying not collect dead ones. Why kill a butterfly to name it when you already know its name? Why pin yourself down before you've gotten started flying?

He felt more than a trace of panic when he went into the kitchen where Dove was making a veal stew and she turned to him and said, "Let's have a baby" and he replied, "Let's not." Luckily his father came in from his bedroom. He looked a little better. "In the hospital I felt like a nail driven into cement," he said, drinking a beer with a sandwich Dove had made for him. Dove drew Thad out onto the porch.

"I just worry you'll go off to Chicago and marry Emily because she's rich and you won't have to work."

"No, I'm thinking of not going to my last year of high school but moving right into college. The principal said I could do it."

As usual when tormented and the weather was right he had gone swimming in a big deep pool in this river not far down from the farm. He had written a paper for biology class about this hole and its large brown trout population. The teacher in turn gave the paper to the editors of a Michigan trout fishing magazine without his permission which irked him. As he expected he was pestered by anglers right from the beginning of the season but steadfastly refused to divulge its whereabouts saying that it would be like giving away his girlfriend. The fish census Thad made was surprising in that this large pool in the river, about thirty yards by twenty yards, held over a hundred brown trout with over half being mature and fairly sizable and a half dozen very large, three over ten pounds taking up residence as far as possible from each other. They were not alarmed by him so he could study them at close quarters. The anglers pestered him because every trout fisherman wishes to catch a brown on fly over five pounds and one of ten pounds would be a lifetime trophy. Being born and raised in the middle of the river made Thad since childhood a rather more bookish angler in that he would fish a short time for as many as ninety days in a row.

Entering the outskirts of Chicago with Emily he was revisited by some of the same feelings he had experienced sprawled out on the tarmac at Meigs Field Airport after his long swim down. It was the recurrent image from a dream of the grandest river of all, the Gulf Stream, the ocean river, so immense it couldn't be seen across, moving from the Florida Gulf through the Atlantic Northeast up past Great Britain, the current profoundly affecting the European climate. He had imagined that if he were ever fatally ill he would like to slip into the ocean river far to the south and swim with the current until he disappeared. His present moody distress however was singularly down-to-earth. When he was in the ninth grade a few years back his parents had become quite worried about his swimming obsession and had arranged a meeting with the school counselor since there was no professional *mind doctor* in the area where mental difficulties no matter how prevalent were not viewed as worth spending money on. Thad viewed the counselor as a stiff, preposterous snot from Ann Arbor who in the American poetry class he taught loathed Walt Whitman, whom Thad loved. The session went poorly and was in fact traumatic to Thad. The counselor ridiculed his love of water and swimming. Did he expect to earn a livelihood from water? Thad was close to losing his temper but caught them all off guard by saying yes, he intended to become a hydrologist, a scientist of water. They backpedaled a bit but some damage was done. Out of resentment he kept himself distant from his parents for a couple of weeks. How could they have put him through this humiliation? Of all the jobs in the world why was his love of swimming in question? Of course parents worry about children but he was confident he could make a fine living out of his love of water. He certainly wouldn't permit any more ridicule. When the counselor tried to greet him in the high school hallway he looked away. When the man shouted "be polite" he bellowed back "fuck you." He was promptly reported to the principal but he and Thad were trout fishing friends and the principal was allowed to fish anywhere in the prime locations on the farm. The principal patiently explained that a student couldn't be allowed to yell "fuck you" at a teacher-counselor and Thad was remorseful, promising to write an apology. However the whole experience made him swim longer and harder and with additional reading he added swimming the length of France's Rhône River to his ambitions. He would certainly become a hero to French girls. On a trip to Ann Arbor he had seen the movie *Jules and Jim* and the wonderful actress Jeanne Moreau apparently had none of the chirrupy chipmunk aspects of American girls. At present as they fully entered Chicago all he wanted to do was be alone in his little room-and-a-half quarters and not hear any more of Emily's normally excusable prattle about the future, an obsession of students that deterred them from exercising any level of attention on the present. Thad tended to be a bit anal. If the weather was passable he would work on the farm four hours each morning, swim four hours in the afternoon, and read four hours in the evening on the science of water. The local librarian was helpful describing all local young males as "dolts and louts." They unloaded and unpacked his bags and he was disappointed that he was to continue on to Winnetka with Emily and have dinner with her parents. He simply wanted to be alone which had been the habit of most of his lifetime on the farm where the loudest of noises were birds and occasionally farm machinery though the rumble of a tractor lacked irritation. This rural background made him ill prepared for the sheer noisiness of modern culture, say a Chicago traffic jam. When they finally entered Emily's neighborhood he felt a bit of dread at the grandeur of the homes. When they pulled into Emily's circular drive she had phoned ahead and her parents were on the porch of a very large home he recognized as English Tudor style. He wondered why in God's name a family of three needed a home and manicured grounds of this grand size. Something similar was happening near his home in northern Michigan in select locations where wealthy people from Detroit, Chicago, and Indiana built oversized and expensive summer homes far beyond any space possibly needed. This was what an economic text from Thorstein Veblen called "conspicuous consumption": the urge of rich people to show off their wealth. In the vast living room John Scott told him that the fireplace had been moved over from Sussex where it had been built in the fourteenth century for an ancestor of his wife. Thad thought it should be left where it belonged but then chided himself for being snarky.

Out in the backyard there was a very large assortment of barbecue equipment similar to that of Laurie's father Friendly Frank. John Scott had been slow cooking a fine-smelling brisket all day, a "Kansas brisket" he said. Thad wondered about this cultural pride in big barbecue operations when most of the nation managed with small Webers. It starts with boys insisting on the best bicycle and then moves on to cars he thought. He talked at length with Emily's mother who was far too worried about crime despite living in a fortress. This seemed typical of rich people, the functional motto being "I must be completely safe." He couldn't remember feeling more out of place at a home. At the houses of his schoolmates and friends the odors were of kerosene from heaters, cow manure and milk from the barn and cream separators and always a trace of mud and chicken shit from the barnyard. When he would visit a girl he would take a bouquet from his mother's flower garden which would delight everyone and was rare, as flowers were deemed impractical for a workaday farm. It was all hard work and fried potatoes.

He drank too much wine but maintained his balance which was family tradition. To drink and pretend it had little influence until it was pretty much true. He had grown up with the habit of thinking about the cost of everything, typical of people who have to turn the soil into dollars and cents, people who are free of the abstractions money can twirl in our sorry heads. How many bushels of tomatoes or sweet corn will it take to get the house painted? We're better off doing it ourselves in spare time that doesn't actually exist. So you paint after dinner until summer dark.

Thad was eating the delicious brisket and drinking goblets of French red wine and not listening to Emily talking with her mother Elisabeth who had just had a call from her sister who lived in Paris. This aunt wanted to trade with Emily her apartment on rue Vaneau for ten days in August for her quarters in the house that had been her own as a girl. Thad could easily see that the conversation was set up to get his attention and he would likely be expected to join Emily. Emily and her mother got up to clear the table and when they were out of earshot John Scott stared at Thad.

"What do you think?" he asked.

"I have my court case that time in August."

"I know that. You should let me get even for you. I can floor that shitheel easily."

"It's personal."

"You could fly to Paris four days late then spend some extra time in a hotel."

"I feel I'm getting in over my head. I need to go to work and earn some money."

"You'll be working your entire life. You'll be on salary for this trip. Why turn down a free trip to France?"

"I'm not accustomed to this life."

"If you ever become the father of a daughter you'll understand my request. She's attractive, but also inattentive and innocent. I see her talking to strangers all the time downtown. She doesn't understand the nature of predatory men. I worry myself to the point of illness about her. You could easily keep an eye on her. She told me that there are some rivers in France you want to swim. This is a perfect opportunity."

"Let me think." Thad was wondering how he was ever going to get anywhere by himself. He had finally made Chicago but not New York, or the incredible new aquarium near San Francisco. Right now he could barely buy a ticket home without digging into his meager savings. "I'd have to be a few days late because of the trial."

"She can wait," John Scott said with obvious pleasure that he had won.

July moved slowly, with worries that came from phone calls from his mother about his father's postinjury depression. The warehouse work was hard but he enjoyed burning up his body with exhaustion as many men do, as the fatigue modulated the worries. The first day of work he was tested by cleaning up and rebagging a pallet of sacks of fertilizer many of which had broken open in transit. He had to wear a gas mask and it was very hot. Everyone seemed to know of his relationship with the owner's daughter but then Emily had dropped him off at work several times after they had disregarded the landlady's rules against sleepovers.

When they reached the place they had a little chitchat about perennials with the landlady, particularly peonies, her obsession. They went inside and quickly made love after which he rested his head on her lower spine and studied the flowers out the window through the crack of her ass, a lovely vision. His mind was a not unpleasant welter of water baby thoughts. From a classic naturalist's point of view their survival was up to them. They seemed undisturbed by large fish themselves but maybe as human babies they came onto earth at seven pounds, much too large for trout food. A passing otter also didn't make them shy and stopped a moment to play. However when the local osprey flew over the water babies they shied from his shadow and gathered under Thad's body for protection. Perhaps the primitive avian intelligence didn't recognize them as human babies. Thad questioned whether with his interest in the natural sciences he had the right to keep this momentous secret for himself. A number of academics came by to fish each summer but mostly of the literary type. Writers seem drawn to the grace and peace of fly-fishing. He liked one in particular, a poet and graduate student from Michigan State working in despair on his PhD because he needed money for a burgeoning family of three children. It seemed a mistake to Thad if it depressed him that much. He drank too much from a flask and occasionally tumbled in the water but had a wading staff and was strong enough to right himself. He had promised Thad he would send him an ancient Sufi essay called "The Logic of Birds and Fishes" but it never came and Thad couldn't trace it through his own library or the Internet. He thought that the only angler to be trusted with a secret was an old professor emeritus of natural history from the University of Michigan in Ann Arbor. The poet would blab, but the old professor might be overwhelmed and still keep the secret. Like many he usually arrived for the grasshoppers in August. The more Thad thought about it he became slightly ashamed of himself for not sharing with the scientific community even if the secret was ultimately misused. He was sure he had observed vestigial gill openings under their chins but they also ascended to the surface quickly every few minutes for air like marine mammals. Obviously at the time they felt vulnerable as they would suck in quick voluminous breaths. The mystery was the origin and he doubted any spiritual aspect unlike Tooth. If they see an aborted fetus or an abandoned sick baby do they take care of it? It's unlikely he would ever know.

So he worked hard and became well liked by the other employees. When John Scott visited he paid Thad no particular attention, knowing that it would make things harder for him as in *teacher's pet.* If he showed up at lunch he would buy a sandwich from the cart out front just like everyone else. It was operated by an old Polish lady who made grand sandwiches and sometimes plastic bowls of pierogies with butter and sour cream. If you're truly hungry from hard work a liver sausage on rye with onions and hot mustard would take you through until dinner if the sausage quantity was ample. The ease of lunch hour reminded him of the best times with his mother talking at the kitchen table with taciturn Dad eating on the porch if weather permitted. He had that "thousand-yard stare" of many Vietnam veterans as if he were struggling to balance a past that was still too vivid to be truly the past. Thad and his mother would chat away about what they had been reading but go back to work outside promptly at 1 p.m. Often lunch was his favorite, a grilled sharp cheddar cheese with raw onion. In season they would eat a pile of fresh radishes and tiny green onions dipped in butter and salt. When Dad got home from the hospital Dove fixed him soups because he had lost teeth in the attacks. He told Thad one day that what he missed most in Vietnam was the Mexican food he had grown up on in Texas. He concluded by saying that when you're shooting at people and getting shot at food can be a big morale item, something that anchors you on earth in the horror and absurdity of war.

He returned to the theme of what happens to people who are witnesses to the miraculous? Right now in late July in Chicago he was terribly homesick without knowing what it meant. He knew he could never marry Emily because it meant a lifetime of being bullied by John Scott. Having no impulse to push people around himself he had no real understanding of bullies. Right now while moving more pallets hither and yon with a forklift he was homesick for weeding tomatoes though they likely didn't need it because they had put down a lot of straw mulch. There was definitely a lump in his throat and a deep need to see his water babies and he doubted whether he was able to get on a plane for Paris. When people ready their minds for their first trip abroad they often speculate if they'll ever get back home.

At the end of the first week in August he was in a courtroom and could not imagine a less pleasant place except a hospital. The young lawyer who advised them said that Friendly Frank and his lawyer would likely go for a longish delay but doubted that the *left wing* judge would allow it because the accusations against Friendly Frank had piled up and public opinion had turned resoundingly against him. In fact the court-room was jammed as they say and early on in the testimony when Friendly Frank said he struck Thad with a club because he caught him "molesting his daughter," Laurie screamed, "Dad, that's a lie, you're the molester," which was stunning. The judge absurdly enough told the jury to ignore what Laurie had screamed. Their lawyer did his job and even got a hold of the doctor Thad met fishing at the river mouth who described in lurid detail Thad's balloon face. After three days of blabber Friendly Frank was sentenced to thirty days in jail which was immediately appealed.

When Thad talked to the doctor that evening the man asked if he was willing to go to Ann Arbor to try out for the University of Michigan swim coach. Thad felt obligated and Mother drove him down early the next morning. Before they left they walked upstream until they reached the pond. Thad stripped, dove in, and quickly met nose-to-nose with a water baby which he gently lifted up for his mother to see. He heard a shriek and lowered the baby back to the water. When he came up his mother was pale and he slowly repeated what Tooth had to say. She shivered though it wasn't cold and began to cry. "I can't handle this," she said, and they walked to their makeshift ferry and the car. They were a half hour into the trip before she could talk rationally. He said he had no real idea about anything, not being a spiritual creature himself. He had to somewhat believe Tooth because he had no other choice. We are rational creatures and he readily admitted that it somewhat limited us. What were they? He had no idea except that they were water babies, like the old story. He imagined that they finally and slowly left this area and crawled up on the beach where they could be picked up by the many people desperate to adopt.

Ann Arbor was a no-brainer. They met with the swimming coach, went over to the pool, where Thad's *perfect* swimmer's build was admired. Thad swam the hundred as best he could and the coach and gaggle of assistant coaches were ecstatic and offered him a full scholarship because he broke the Big Ten record by several seconds. He felt nothing other than being relieved of the onus of John Scott's bullying. "Free at last," he whispered to himself. Of course it wasn't Emily's fault any more than Laurie's father was her fault. Who knows why men become bullies? It likely starts young. He had told Bone that he couldn't hit Pudge because she was female and he yelled, "Bullshit," but then she frequently beat him into the ground. Of course there are also female bullies though not as many.

His mother drove him out to the airport to save money and he flew to Chicago first class. He had never flown first class and couldn't see the difference except the seat was wider and a drink was free. In Chicago he met Emily at the American Airlines Admirals Club. They had a crappy fast-food lunch and boarded the Paris flight, taking the train out to the international terminal in late afternoon. They flew business class which embarrassed Thad when he found out how much more expensive it was than tourist class. "That's Dad," Emily said. "You can't stop him from trying to spoil me."

They ate a mediocre meal, and Thad slept several hours from fatigue after the extreme exertion of his test swim.

The flight seemed to take forever though he was still surprised when he saw France below him out the window early in the morning. After customs the driver John Scott used in Paris picked them up. He was amused that rich people had to arrange everything. You couldn't just land in a city and take a cab or subway, it had to be a very nice Renault sedan. On the way in to the apartment they stopped at the Bon Marché food court on the ground floor of the building and loaded up on what Emily called *picnic* food. Her aunt's apartment looked down into the prime minister's gardens and you could easily have the illusion of eating outside. The thing Emily always dreaded most about being in Paris with her father was his penchant for semiformal lunches and dinners at the best restaurants in town. She didn't want to be intimidated and had appalled her father years before in her midteens by saying she "loathed" Le Taillevent. Consequently she shopped like a maniac buying wine, veal chops, a dozen cheeses, and showed Thad the herring where he grabbed ten kinds. They were exhausted and silly because the bread looked so good they bought several kinds.

The apartment was large and airy with a wall of windows looking down in the garden in back. It was on the third floor and the furniture looked delicate and expensive to Thad. The bedroom was somewhat absurd with a canopied bed and Emily said that her aunt dealt in French antiques she shipped to New York and Chicago and occasionally to Los Angeles. He was hungry after the pathetic airline breakfast and busied himself unpacking groceries. To a totally inexperienced man all of the cheeses stank but were delicious, especially the Vacheron and Époisses. After some herring and ham he threw himself facedown on the bed and woke in two hours with nude Emily beside him. She made coffee and then they took her favorite walk through the Luxembourg Gardens, stopping to see the lovely dwarf fruit trees, then way down to the Jardin des Plantes for the flowers, back up Montparnasse, stopping at Café Select to split a bottle of Brouilly, an excellent summer wine. It was a soft, sunny afternoon and he couldn't comprehend his melancholy except for the recurrent image of the way the water babies rose slowly from being nestled on the bottom to the surface for air. They couldn't be true but there they were. They especially seized him when he and Emily sat in the little park across Raspail from the Laetitia Hotel where city employees were busy transplanting flowers. What a fine job, he thought. Why should everyone want to be a big shot? Why not just plant flowers in cities for likely low wages and make everyone with eyes happy.

On the way home he bought a map of France from a kiosk and spread it out on the living room floor with the thought that there might be water babies in the Seine but more likely in a trout river in his *Rivers of Earth* book that was down in an area called the Massif Central. He made notes on a half dozen rivers he might want to swim in and asked Emily how they could get around. Right away she said "car and driver" and this irked him because he noticed that the receipt for picnic supplies was nearly four hundred euros including sixty bucks for a single bottle of wine. She sensed his irritation and said when he made up his mind precisely they'd go to a travel agent and get train tickets. She wanted to throw in the Guadalquivir near Seville, Spain, her favorite European river because of the poet Federico García Lorca. She loved his work and read Spanish well. She had visited Seville, Barcelona, and Madrid with her parents when she was twelve and was quite swept away, especially by the music and art museums.

Paris became overly warm, nearly sweltering in the afternoon, so they got up very early to walk though most of the time Thad walked down to a kiosk for the *Herald Tribune* for Emily and walked by himself, always over to the Luxembourg Gardens for a natural world fix. At 10 a.m. when it opened Emily could manage the museum straight down the street to the river. Thad was amazed at the difference between seeing the actual painting rather than a print out of an art book. It was almost uncomfortable walking around a corner in the museum and there was an actual van Gogh. When they got home, had a modest picnic, made love, and peeled their bodies apart in the heat, he shyly admitted to her that he was thinking of learning to be a painter. It seemed to go with swimming. She liked this because she had no idea what he could ultimately do with swimming. Not that he needed to win her trust but she deeply sensed his suspicion of wealth in general. Since she was born with it she barely noticed it. When she was little they went to San Francisco on a private railroad car.

The very next day Paris was a hundred degrees and she hastily bought train tickets for Marseilles and made some hotel reservation calls. Thad loved the TGV ride of over 150 mph, and all of the views of hills, farms, vineyards, the Rhône River. He was curious about the city of Lyon but she couldn't help much having only been there once with her father on business. She said her dad had said it was the best eating town in France and the agriculture capital. Thad made a mental note to swim through the town at some point, also to run up the steep hill for no particular reason.

In Marseilles they took a local train and rented a car in Arles, driving to the Nord-Pinus, a hotel in the city square where Emily had once stayed with her parents. Thad liked it because their room was so large compared to apartment rooms. In the relative cool of the evening they walked the few blocks down to the colosseum which was about two thousand years old and still in use for bullfights. In the middle of the arena two cats were making love and a group of young French students cheered them on. They had a light dinner at Le Galoubet and a long difficult evening in the room.

"I don't think you want to marry me" is how it began.

"I'm almost eighteen and you're nineteen, which seems to be jumping the gun," is how he responded, a slight knot in his throat. He called the desk and ordered a double vodka on ice because Emily poured herself a glass of wine from a bottle she had packed in her satchel. It was a sixty-dollar bottle and he admitted to himself it was delicious. Why does the good stuff have to be so expensive?

A stupid question probably. Things didn't go well. The two vodkas made him argumentative. Out of the blue he said dramatically that he hoped to die alone in a small log cabin on a river. She broke into tears. It is a terrible thing when one's love far exceeds the other's. There was no way to comfort her. She was inconsolable. He had done violence to her fantasy life which clearly included him. He sat down at the window hearing her sniffling behind him. He viewed early marriage as banal as swimming the English Channel. He felt an absurd agitation. You go on vacation and end up sitting looking out the window. Her pillow actually became wet with tears. He finally couldn't resist her rump in its summer skirt and making love slowed but didn't abolish the tears. She said, "All I want to do is take care of you," to which he couldn't respond. It made him miss the caustic aspects of Laurie's character, an extended schoolboy crush her father had destroyed. Girls readily ignored the spirit of adventure biologically invested in young males. He adored Emily but doubted that this constituted enduring love. There was a world out there to swim through.

Close after a warm dawn they left the hotel, surprised how few French get up early. Armed with maps they made their way south. He swam across the mouth of the Rhône and back, drying off with a hotel towel. He was totally intoxicated with the Camargue and its virtual explosion of the natural. They hugged the Mediterranean heading west. Thad studied the thousands of birds through Emily's opera glasses. He couldn't have imagined this place with his preconceptions of Europe. They stopped on the road and watched a group of cowboys on white and gray horses with long poles with sharp points chasing a herd of cattle. Emily quickly figured out that the cattle were fighting bulls. One charged the sturdy fence where Thad stood. The anger of the bull made him feel good, bellowing, blowing snot, red-eyed, and obviously wanting to kill him. It exhilarated him as did the vast expanse of pasture, much of it subirrigated so that they were running through shallow water flushing birds. He swam all day while Emily sunbathed and read a Swedish mystery which seemed to hope to make up for the fact that not much happens there. Thad saw this as a good thing and hoped to swim in Sweden someday late in a summer when presumably the water would be warm enough. He loved those aerial photos of fjords. Meanwhile his intoxication with the estuarine area made him giddy. Should he ever become a hydrologist he hoped to visit all of the great estuarine areas of the world. Their fertility of life was miraculous, the gift of water.

They found a little restaurant on the edge of an actual garden for lunch and at one table a dark man was playing guitar hauntingly. With her rudimentary French Emily found out from the waitress that the man was a *gitane,* a local Gypsy, and he was playing his people's music which Thad thought was overwhelmingly beautiful, so much so that he felt teary. He held Emily's hand. She was also overcome and he reminded himself that Emily could get him around to all the many estuarine areas on earth. Did it have to be a question of virtual captivity? If you are not jealous of your freedom who will be for you?

They drove farther west toward Montpellier along the coast and Thad had a long swim in the Mediterranean itself. Afterward Emily explained that train travel tended to span out like a wheel from Paris and lateral movement tended to be more limited. If they wanted to see both the Guadalquivir and the Loire on this trip they'd have to do some driving rather than just take the train. That was fine by him.

They returned to Arles fairly exhausted for one more night, a brief dinner at Le Galoubet, and a night of vivid dreams about death. He got up for a glass of water and watched a drunk stumble across the town square making a moaning sound. In periods of extreme loneliness we don't know a thing about life and death and the reality of water consoles us. In school he had long thought that history, the study of it, was an instrument of terror. Reading about either the American Indians or slaves can make you physically ill. He wanted a life as free as possible from other people, thus simply staying on the island was tempting. The possibility of stopping people from doing what they do to other people seemed out of the question. Congressmen die in bed.

In the clear light of morning with cool heads it seemed best to go to the Loire first, stopping in Saumur for Emily to see the horses, Thad to swim the river, then fly to the Guadalquivir from Lyon to Seville. Emily was a good driver and he liked staring out the window and dozing, sometimes jerked alert by his water babies, the primary fact of his life whether he wished to admit it or not. It seemed comic to him that people desire miracles but when they get them it adds an extremely confusing element to life.

Maybe Lazarus didn't want to come back to life.

They reached Saumur in time for the scheduled horse event which pleased Emily. It was a strange kind of formation riding, very skilled, with lines of the horses weaving in and out of each other. Saumur is a military college and the riders redefined stiffness except they would jump the horses very high without stirrups and Thad was aware of the level of difficulty which was way up there. The horses and riders seemed to genuinely like each other which was critical. When he was a boy his mother who was drastically allergic to dogs bought him a small horse, really a pony, who acted like a dog, sleeping in the yard. Each morning when he awoke at dawn the horse was looking in the window and he reached out and petted it which the horse obviously liked. They'd hike around the island together and the horse who hated its saddle loved to be ridden bareback. Naturally it liked to swim and the curious feeling of swimming while riding the back of a horse stuck with him.

After the Saumur horse event they drove down the Loire and checked into lavish rooms at the Le Prieuré Château-Hôtel in Chenehutte-les-Tuffeaux on a hill above the Loire. Thad was tempted to hike in the forest surrounding the hotel but on the parapet in front he was pulled by the river. On the way from Saumur they had a near miss with a Land Rover towing a speedboat. Thad guessed that the driver was drunk. They checked in and Emily asked about swimming. "Madame, there are no beaches in the area," the desk clerk responded.

Emily did a pantomime of driving and pointed to Thad. The desk clerk gave him an appraising eye as if he was nuts. Out the window you could see the Loire far below and she drew a little map. Thad was anxious to get in the water so they didn't take time to unpack.

Down on the edge of the river Emily could see the Land Rover launching the speedboat a hundred yards upstream and had the icy feeling she always had around drunks. It took off passing too close to a fisherman who shook his fist and shouted. Thad stripped and dove in heading toward the river's middle in broad strokes. It was a warmish noon and Emily felt drowsy. She craned her neck and could see some hotel employees watching the crazy Americans from the parapet high above them.

It didn't take long. Accidents never do. There is a stop-time, slow-motion aspect to them whether it is automobiles colliding or airplanes falling from the sky or collisions on a football field that cause severe injuries. The speedboat was roaring at high speed in wide circles. Thad saw it heading toward him and so did Emily who pointlessly screamed. Thad rose up in the water and waved his arms but evidently wasn't seen. The boat struck his body head-on with a horrifying thud and the two girls aboard began screaming and there was a scream from far up on the parapet of the hotel. The boat turned around and headed toward Thad in the water, hitting him in the head. More screams from the girls onboard. One grabbed his hair and they towed him ashore where Emily was running down the brambly bank. The angry fisherman was on his cell phone. Thad was in a dream state thinking he might have seen a water baby in the Loire. He was vomiting blood profusely because the bow of the boat had hit him in the middle of the chest. The blood felt hot and sticky on his chest and Emily knelt beside him. Now the fisherman was there and holding up Thad's shoulders so he wouldn't drown on his own blood. The desk clerk from the hotel arrived and yelled *"vite!"* into the cell phone. The two men manning the speedboat wandered toward their car and took off leaving their passengers behind.

The green grass around Thad was wet with red blood. Emily was a mess from hugging him and then there was some dead time with Thad gurgling, the passengers sobbing. The ambulance finally arrived and the attendants' main worry was Thad's heart might be being compressed by his fractured ribs. Thad was unconscious and Emily was sure he was dead until he moaned loudly while being loaded. She rode in the ambulance and made a hysterical call to her father. At the small hospital in Saumur a military doctor determined that the injuries were too grave to be treated locally and included five fractured ribs, a burst spleen, a broken back, a slight skull fracture from when the boat rescued him and hit his head. Late that evening when he was somewhat stabilized a helicopter took him up to Lyon, partly because John Scott had made calls and with his connections the embassy asserted the best place for the time being to treat Thad was Lyon. Thad had lapsed into unconsciousness for a while but was awake when he reached Lyon where the first medical process was to relieve pressure on his heart. John Scott arrived in Lyon the next day with a consul of the government and the plan was perhaps five more days in Lyon and then a hospital jet would fly Thad to

Grand Rapids, Michigan, an obvious advantage to having lots of money.

On the interior, this is the kind of injury that makes you think your life is over. He developed pneumonia and his frenzied and fevered nights were haunted by the water babies and severe chest pain. He was flown to Grand Rapids the last week of August and was home at the farm, physically a ghost of himself, in mid-September.

On a warm day in late September his mother, Tooth, Dove, Emily, and Laurie helped him down the island to the water baby pond. They packed sandwiches and sat there on the bank on a day that was simply glittery and clear though a storm out of the west was predicted, the first Alberta Clipper that came out of the Northwest in the fall. He had been having a modest quarrel with Emily, insisting she should go back to Sarah Lawrence for the fall term. He obviously had plenty of caretakers.

The women left him at the pond, a mistake, and went back to the farm to pick the remains of the bounteous tomato crop before the predicted frost that would come after the windstorm. The girls would return for him in the afternoon.

He sat there staring into the pond and was delighted when a water baby rounded for air and then one stuck its face out of the water and stared at him, swirling in what he believed was a greeting. He had spent a great deal of time pondering suicide because of the pain and the fact that his life was in shambles. The athletic scholarship would be withdrawn from the University of Michigan. He had his grandpa's .38 caliber pistol hidden in his room but he finally couldn't bear to bring his mother grief. He couldn't bear his big collection of pain pills because they made him feel loopy and lifeless. Pain itself was better than those. So he drifted with the pain, feeling also the maddening itch between his partial chest cast the doctor had somewhat reduced in size to help his mobility. Now that it was apparent that he would live and could walk however haltingly he hoped to go back to Lyon to see his main nurse. She was a farm girl just as he was a farm boy and they had talked in his fractional French and her pathetic English and when he left they kissed. In the French hospital Emily became the sister he never had. He didn't know what to do about it but any sense of romance was absent. Since he was brought home he drifted far from the improbable accident to the future, which had become inconsequential, to the past that was equally so to the present, moment by moment, which utterly seized him. He suspected it might have been caused by the head blow but the merest filament of reality seemed to be livid and glittered.

The pond beckoned him though he knew if the chest cast got wet the cast would disintegrate. He suddenly was bored by all things medical what with being over-exposed. Sitting there he suddenly tipped over gently and rolled into the water. Being enveloped by water for the first time in a month utterly delighted him.

There were thirteen to be exact. They smothered around his head and shoulders, kissing him, poking at his chest cast with curiosity, then pushing him toward the channel exit to the river from the pond. It occurred to him that they might have been waiting to migrate thinking he might wish to join them. Why stay here in the winter when the pond might freeze to the bottom like many bodies of shallow water in northern Michigan?

They drifted along the bottom as if getting to know each other again but he was being pulled decidedly toward the channel exit. He knew it was wrong, that in a short time all of the women, including his mother, would return to guide his crippled body back home. But he couldn't resist these otherworldly creatures any more than early disciples could resist Jesus in favor of supporting their families. When he was in critical care in Lyon the possibility of death became less then alarming. You sense that death is possibly near and on more than one occasion his farm girl nurse shook him awake. He had a trace of sepsis, blood poisoning, that the doctors thought came from the river water mixed with the severity of his injury. Sepsis is often fatal but his body was young and vital.

Now he was thinking a sense of mortality was pervasive in the natural world. Is the inevitability somehow in the blood to the point that animals don't bother thinking about it or fearing it? Years ago an old neighbor lady asked him to *put down* the very old sick dog she owned and the dog's eyes seemed to comprehend the nature of the discussion. Farm families extinguished their own animals rather than going through the expense of a veterinarian. Thad had gone on walks for years with this dog. Whenever he passed the house the dog would run out and greet him from its lair under the porch then trot with him along the river or into the forest. But when he looked the dog in the eyes the pistol in his coat pocket seemed to weigh a hundred pounds. He simply couldn't be the dog's exit from Earth. They walked to town with the dog tottering along and for long stretches Thad carried it. He used his own money at the vet's, an exorbitant amount, he thought, fifty dollars of money he had earned at fifty cents an hour. He carried the dog back to the old woman in a black plastic sack and buried the dog in a flower bed because her name was *Flower.* Thad's mother was allergic to dogs so he never got to own one. The question was whether on the long walk to town if the dog had any idea what was going to happen to it? It had seemed particularly merry that day, by extension maybe they understand death better than we, a sense of beginning, middle, and end which they regard with passionless aplomb. It was all sedate as the migration the water babies seemed urged toward. Or maybe they were taking him to the veterinarian he thought with a smidgen of paranoia.

The cast had begun to disintegrate in the water and the freedom of movement was wonderful though it came with extra pain. He was surrounded by them as he eased out the channel, thinking that he had missed grasshopper season and the chance to drown Friendly Frank. He would have to leave it up to Tooth during deer season when she said she would "pop his skull" with her 30.06 rifle.

He knew that the women would be in a state of shock when they returned to find him not there. Now he was fairly gliding down the river with his friends around him flittering this way and that as if in play.

By the time he passed through town the women had returned to the pond site and within an hour the State Police dive team were there, of course finding nothing in the pond and there was no place else it was sensible to look once the local contact, the sheriff, told them that earlier in the summer Thad had swum to Chicago.

By nightfall Thad had reached the mouth of the river where the winds were coming in very strong, over fifty knots, off Lake Michigan. The waves were growing moment by moment. They were already a dozen feet high and the river's strong current barely got him through. The troughs of waves in Lake Michigan are without tidal influence and so are much narrower than in the ocean thus the swimming or boaters tend to get relentlessly slammed. You move upward with the water, then are tossed or flipped. His little friends clung to him as if they were all glue. After midnight on his westward course he was exhausted and cold to the point that they had to buoy him up in unison. Throughout the night he was mercilessly tossed and trashed and by dawn when the storm began to subside he was more dead than alive. By midmorning the Coast Guard found him forty miles out. And when they dropped the harness and stretcher the volunteer going down the rope was sure he saw that the victim seemed to be surrounded by thickish fish of about a dozen pounds apiece. This mystified him but he pushed it aside in favor of the duties of the moment. After they raised him to the chopper the medic determined that Thad was nearly dead from hypothermia but recoverable.

At a private sanitarium outside Chicago John Scott was speaking with the psychiatrist.

"We don't seem to have many options for keeping him alive," John Scott said quizzically.

"Lock and key. Extreme supervision. Very expensive. This is indefinite. It's ultimately up to him."

"Only the light touch will work in the long run," John Scott said.

In three weeks Thad was home again and recovering. His father and Dove kept an eye on him full-time, backed up by Tooth. It was hard but by the end of October the four of them were at the pond with a length of binder twine tied between Thad and Dove. He saw no signs of life and wondered what his miniature friends thought when the helicopter picked him up out in Lake Michigan. It was one of those spectral, glistening, sunny, early fall days after a light rain, warmish with all of the collective fall odors flooding the nose. They hadn't sat there for more than fifteen minutes before Dove shrieked, "Look." The thirteen water babies came surging in the channel, made one circle of the pond on the surface then went back out the channel into the river. Apparently, he thought, they had come to say good-bye. He heard his father breathe deeply and mutter "What?" Tooth began singing. They belonged where they were.

That evening he was back at his desk staring out at the twilight, wondering how far they swam to find the warmer winter water they needed. He was rereading *The Rivers of Earth* deciding that he must stay alive to greet them next spring. He turned out the light and lay down after rereading the Amazon and Nile chapters for the umpteenth time. You could not swim the lower Nile or a hippo might very well bite you in half like they did crocodiles. Hippos had a pride of ownership over their rivers. Stay out, mine, they said. He dreaded the upcoming winter. Emily was trying to persuade him to come to Costa Rica with her but she was being pushy. He had called Laurie that morning but she didn't want to see him anymore. She felt *betrayed.* He couldn't blame her. Emily had a college project of a botanical nature in Costa Rica and said he would love the water there especially around Flamingo Bay where there were conical volcanic rocks upthrusting from the ocean. It all made him feel the injustice of money in the world. The message was, if you're poor stay home, the only real temptation was that he had never swum in the tropics so perhaps his pride was misplaced. Why freeze his ass off as usual on the farm cross-country skiing every day. He felt mentally victimized by the miraculous. Life would have been easier without the water babies. The world lost its top with their appearance. He felt the lumpishness of a coming depression. He turned the light back on and read about Costa Rica in his old shabby *Britannica* he had bought at a Grand Rapids yard sale. He recalled what his father, who was susceptible, had said about depression. Early in the process you always had to have your antennae out. You had to cook or boil yourself down late in the evening when you're too desperate to lie still and see what's there deep in your soul. That was easy for Thad.

The young scholar from Michigan State said that poets and novelists were whores for language, that they would give anything for something good. Thad easily accepted the idea that he was a whore for swimming, the only activity that gave him total pleasure and a sense of absolutely belonging on Earth, especially swimming in rivers with the current carrying your water-enveloped body along at its own speed. It was bliss to him so why shouldn't he be obsessed? And if Emily wanted to take him swimming in Costa Rica it was only another kind of whoredom. What was at issue except pride? The classic "I can't be bought" but then I can. He would anyway end up selling his life for a job like anyone else, including his dad putting out oil well fires or his mother donating her life to the farm. It's just what people did. He could even imagine doing so at the age Grandpa had been when he died, eighty-one, an old man heading downriver. A teacher had told him that for most of his life the great James Joyce had to be supported by a woman named Sylvia Beach.

But he didn't say where she had gotten the money to begin with. Was there truly dirty money? Or was it purified by rotation and use.

Frankly he didn't mind being a whore. In the past decades the word had lost its power. He slipped off his nightclothes after looking at the reflection of a big moon in the river. Leaving the room he heard a suspicious click in the door and he accurately guessed it was a device Dove had devised to let her know if he left the room. He quickly passed through the dining room and out the front door. From the front door he could see Dove standing by the kitchen table talking to his parents then moving hurriedly off. Maybe he was just going to the bathroom down the hall? But Dove had to check. By then Thad had trotted down the yard and had dove in the river. He was merciful to those he loved and just swam down the length of the river, pulled himself out by grabbing a branch, then trotted back to the house by a well-worn path, memorized to avoid stubbing toes on roots. They met him at the front door with his mother weeping and Dove yelling, "God damn you Thad." His dad poured him a shot of whiskey and his mother dried him off with a handful of kitchen towels from a drawer.

It had been an utterly delicious swim, moving downstream toward the moon that glistened both in the sky and on the water.

Back in bed he felt comfortable and totally hopeless. If there was a body of swimmable water nearby he would enter it. It was his nature.

ABOUT THE AUTHOR

Jim Harrison is the author of over thirty books of poetry, nonfiction and, fiction, including *Legends of the Fall, The Road Home, Returning to Earth,* and *The Summer He Didn't Die.* A member of American Academy of Arts and Letters and winner of a Guggenheim Fellowship, he has had work published in twenty-seven languages. Harrison lives in Montana and Arizona.

The employees of Thorndike Press hope you have enjoyed this Large Print book. All our Thorndike, Wheeler, and Kennebec Large Print titles are designed for easy reading, and all our books are made to last. Other Thorndike Press Large Print books are available at your library, through selected bookstores, or directly from us.

For information about titles, please call:
  (800) 223-1244

or visit our Web site at:
  http://gale.cengage.com/thorndike

To share your comments, please write:
  Publisher
  Thorndike Press
  10 Water St., Suite 310
  Waterville, ME 04901